SALMI PASSAGGIATI (1615)

RECENT RESEARCHES IN THE MUSIC OF THE BAROQUE ERA

Robert L. Marshall, general editor

A-R Editions, Inc., publishes six quarterly series—

Recent Researches in the Music of the Middle Ages and Early Renaissance,
Margaret Bent, general editor;

Recent Researches in the Music of the Renaissance,
James Haar and Howard Mayer Brown, general editors;

Recent Researches in the Music of the Baroque Era,
Robert L. Marshall, general editor;

Recent Researches in the Music of the Classical Era,
Eugene K. Wolf, general editor;

Recent Researches in the Music of the Nineteenth and Early Twentieth Centuries,
Jerald C. Graue, general editor;

Recent Researches in American Music,
H. Wiley Hitchcock, general editor—

which make public music that is being brought to light
in the course of current musicological research.

Each volume in the *Recent Researches* is devoted
to works by a single composer or to a single genre of composition,
chosen because of its potential interest to scholars and performers,
and prepared for publication according to the standards that govern
the making of all reliable historical editions.

Correspondence should be addressed:

A-R EDITIONS, INC.
315 West Gorham Street
Madison, Wisconsin 53703

RECENT RESEARCHES IN THE MUSIC OF THE BAROQUE ERA • VOLUME XXXVIII

Francesco Severi

SALMI PASSAGGIATI
(1615)

Edited by Murray C. Bradshaw

A-R EDITIONS, INC. • MADISON

Copyright © 1981, A-R Editions, Inc.

ISSN 0484-0828

ISBN 0-89579-158-7

Library of Congress Cataloging in Publication Data:
Severi, Francesco, ca. 1595-1630.
    Salmi passaggiati.
    (Recent researches in the music of the baroque era ;
v. 38)
    For 1-4 solo voices (SATB) and continuo.
    Figured bass realized for organ.
    Contents: Dixit Dominus : primo tuono —
Confitebor tibi Domine : secondo tuono — Beatus
vir : terzo tuono — [etc.]
    Includes as appendices Dentice's Miserere in
whole or in part in three different versions.
    1. Sacred songs with continuo.   2. Sacred duets
with continuo.   3. Sacred trios with
continuo.   4. Sacred quartets with
continuo.   5. Psalms (Music)   6. Magnificat
(Music) I. Bradshaw, Murray C.   II. Dentice,
Fabrizio, 16th cent. Lamentationi. Miserere.
1981.   III. Title,   IV. Series: Recent researches in
the baroque era ; v. 38.
M2.R238   vol. 38   [M2019.5]   81-14881
ISBN 0-89579-158-7   AACR2

Contents

For Doris

"Nisi enim ab homine memoria teneantur,
soni pereunt, quia scribi non possunt."
Isidore of Seville, *De Musica*
(Gerbert, *Scriptores*, I, 20)

". . . so molto bene che simili Passaggi
si sogliono fare all improviso da i buoni
Cantori che in Roma et altrove ordinariamente
cantano nelle Solennità . . ."
Francesco Severi, *Salmi passaggiati*

Preface

The Composer

In 1828, over 200 years after Severi's music first appeared in print, Giuseppe Baini wrote that "there was, among others, a certain Francesco Severi, a singer in our Chapel [the Sistine], who with the greatest success published various books to help those who lacked inventiveness." Baini continued, "Here is the title of his first book: *Salmi passeggiati* [sic] *per tutte le voci nella maniera che si cantano in roma sopra i falsibordoni*. . . ."[1] Part of Severi's goal in having his *Salmi passaggiati* published was, in his own words, to provide music for "those who have a good as well as a mediocre talent."[2] But the value of the collection goes far beyond this modest, pedagogical aim.

Severi's ten "embellished psalms," published in 1615, are first of all a codification of a practice that was almost always improvised, and one that was extremely widespread in the early years of the seventeenth century. Moreover, the *Salmi passaggiati* is not a treatise on embellishment, of which there were many, but a practical collection of compositions intended for direct use in the liturgy.[3] These pieces are also an invaluable record of the kind of singing done in Rome around 1615. Furthermore, in the introduction to the original publication, the composer made some suggestions about the way he wanted his pieces performed, and his comments can well be applied to other music of that period, as they offer fresh insights into the performances of those days. Finally, in Severi's music, we are on the threshold of modern notation and of the modern "beat" as opposed to the ancient "tactus."

The composer was born in Perugia, in central Italy, around 1595.[4] Not much is known of his early life, but in the preface to his *Salmi passaggiati*, Severi said he studied with Ottavio Catalano, "my master . . . his advice and criticism in the present volume have been of great value to me."[5] Catalano was also the teacher of Niccolò Borboni, who, in turn, was the publisher of Severi's *Salmi passaggiati*.[6]

At an early age Severi joined the household of Cardinal Scipione Borghese, nephew of Pope Paul V, and, as Papal Secretary of State, one of the most powerful men in Rome.[7] Severi dedicated his *Salmi* to this influential prince of the Church, and the Borghese coat-of-arms with Cardinal's hat appears on the volume's title page (see Plate I). As Severi said in his introduction, he received "many benefits and favors" from the Cardinal, including his education in music. The *Salmi*, indeed, were "the fruit of those studies nourished in the princely house of your Excellency [Cardinal Scipione]."

In the dedication of the *Salmi*, Severi stressed his youth. "I recall, most illustrious Lord," he wrote, "that you had little concern about my youthfulness, and so I venture to present to your most illustrious Lordship this small effort, even though habitually the fruit of tender plants is harsh." In the longer introduction "ai lettori" (see below, p. xxii), Severi begged the readers' indulgence for "this first effort of mine, which both in itself and because of the age of the author is immature and imperfect." If Severi was about twenty when the *Salmi* appeared, he would have been born around 1595. He would also have been about eighteen when he entered the Sistine on 31 December 1613.

Although Severi entered the Papal Chapel under the full aegis of the Borghese family, he still underwent some sort of audition, and "having seen his merits and good expectations, the chapelmaster, at this time Arcangelo Crivelli, then presented him with the surplice in the presence of all and with all the customary pomp and circumstance."[8] The archivist of the chapel described Severi as "a eunuch," that is, a castrato. He was among the first castrati to sing in the Pontifical Chapel.

The Chapel diary for 1616 mentions Severi several times. He is described there as singing an *Improperia* and a *Miserere* by Palestrina, as serving the Cardinal Borghese at different times, as being excused now and then for illness, and on 15 August as asking "permission to leave the house because he wished to take communion; this was granted him."[9] He became *puntatore*, or secretary, of the Chapel in 1625.[10] His name also appears in two Sistine manuscripts: in MS 25, a collection made in 1617, his name, "D. Franciscus Severus Perusinus, C[antus]," is written over the first *Agnus Dei*; and on the title page of MS 96, dated 1630, "Franciscus Severus" is listed among the *oxyphoni*, or sopranos.[11]

In the introduction to his *Salmi passaggiati* of 1615, Severi had promised a volume of embellished songs, a promise not fulfilled until 1626, when Paolo Masotti printed the *Arie di Francesco Severi Perugino*. This 1626 print consists of sonnets, arias, madrigals, and romanescas for from one to three voices accompanied by "chitarrone, clavicembalo, & altri simili Instromenti." For some pieces Severi used a guitar accompaniment "alla spagnola." In the introduction to these *Arie*, Severi mentioned his "little book of embellished psalms," the *Salmi passaggiati*. "With every difficulty of *passaggi*, trill, or anything else he might encounter," the singer "will be completely satisfied if he avails himself of the advice I gave on this topic in that same collection of *Salmi*."[12]

A likely reason for delaying publication of the *Arie* for eleven years after the 1615 issue of the *Salmi* was Severi's position in the Sistine Chapel; most members of the Chapel devoted themselves exclusively to sacred music. But this cannot account for the outrage and abusive actions that greeted the printing of the *Arie*. The main reason for this had to be Severi's failure to seek approval for publication from the "Congregatione de' Musici," a group of musicians set up by Pope Urban VIII in 1624 to supervise music in the city of Rome. The result was dramatic. The "congregatione" actually "sent policemen to remove some works of music [probably from the publisher's shop and possibly from the Sistine] which were published by Francesco Severi and which were judged by all to be badly done." However, their actions backfired. "The Pope ordered Msgr. Vulpio to annul the brief that granted faculty to said musicians to do as they had done against Severi."[13]

In addition to the *Salmi* and *Arie*, Severi published two pieces in individual collections. A motet, *Ecce Maria*, appeared in *Lilia campi* (1621; RISM 1621³), a volume of pieces by composers who worked at leading Roman churches—S. Peter's, S. Apollinare, and the Seminario Romano, as well as the Sistine.[14] An Italian piece by Severi, *O di raggi*, was published in *Vezzosetti fiori* (1622; RISM 1622¹¹), a volume that included cembalo and tiorba accompaniments, and, as in Severi's *Arie* of 1626, accompaniment by "la chitarra alla spagnuola." Niccolò Borboni, the publisher of Severi's *Salmi*, also had a piece in this collection. In 1825, G. L. P. Sievers wrote that "a few Masses and motets by [Severi] are still sung," but aside from the *Salmi* and the single motet, no other sacred music seems to have survived.[15]

Francesco Severi died late on Christmas Day, 1630. "He left as heir [the church of] 'la madonna santissima di Costantinopoli.' "[16] Baini noted that Severi was especially devoted "to the most Holy Virgin" and "daily visited her sacred image in S. Maria di Costantinopoli d'Itria" (today known as S. Maria Odigitria).[17] A further connection between Severi and this church was in the person of Matteo Catalano (more than likely a relative of Severi's honored teacher, Ottavio Catalano), who was a member of the archconfraternity that, in 1593, had founded S. Maria di Costantinopoli.

Severi's death was anticipated. Although he died "an hour after dark," Biagio Stocchi, the *puntatore* of the chapel, noted that on that very day his position was passed on to two other singers.[18] He was about thirty-five years old. Late at night on the following day, 26 December, "Francesco Severi was given honorable burial in the church of S. Maria di Costantinopoli."[19] Stocchi added that the "entire college accompanied the body to the church of Santa Maria di Costantinopoli; the singers walked in pairs behind the coffin, as is the usual procedure. When they arrived at the church they sang, as is customary, the 'Libera me, Domine.' "

On 30 December 1630, almost seventeen years after he had entered the Sistine Chapel, "the singers went as a group to the church of the Blessed Virgin of Constantinople, where they sang the Requiem Mass for Francesco Severi, who had died on Christmas Day."[20]

The Popes to whom Severi had devoted his brief life and career were among the most lavish in their support of the arts. All of the members of the Borghese family, Paul V and his two nephews, Cardinal Scipione Borghese and the Prince of Sulmona, constantly fostered new buildings—the Cappella Paolina, the Villa Borghese, numerous palaces, and, perhaps the crowning achievement, the finishing of the *Fabbrica di San Pietro*. "No other family," wrote von Pastor, "has left so many splendid and lasting monuments of itself in Rome as the Borghese."[21] The name of Urban VIII, Matteo Barberini, "is intimately linked with those of artists such as Bernini, Pietro da Cortona, and Andrea Sacchi." Maderna, Castelli, della Greca, and Breccioli were his architects, and "among contemporary painters there were not many who did not get commissions."[22] The spirit of the early baroque, with its drama and fiery emotion, found a vivid expression in the Roman masterworks commissioned by these Popes. The *Salmi passaggiati* of the young Francesco Severi reflects in an equal manner this same spirit of triumph and vigor, of vitality and richness.

The Music

Severi's *Salmi passaggiati* is a collection of ten embellished falsobordone settings of Vesper psalms, the first nine embellishments being based on his own psalm tone settings and the last on an original *Miserere* by Fabrizio (spelled Fabritio in the source of Appendix C) Dentice.[23] Such collections of embellished pieces that are restricted only to one kind of genre and text are rare.[24]

The falsobordone genre originated in the late fifteenth century when composers began to write four-part settings of the ancient Gregorian psalm tones. Despite the similarity of terms, falsobordoni are not at all like the older fauxbourdons. "From the very first, sixth chords are conspicuously absent and root position triads abound; the writing is for four mixed voices (soprano, alto, tenor, bass) and not three equal ones; and all the parts are written out, with none left to improvisation."[25] This "classical" style of the four-part falsobordone eminently summed up the great changes taking place in Western music at the end of the fifteenth century. "The gradual and seemingly inevitable evolution of lucid forms, careful text treatment, choral performance, *a cappella* style, four-part writing, root position triads, and greater awareness of tonality, are all to be seen in this genre."[26]

By the end of the sixteenth century, the genre of the falsobordone had expanded to include not only the classical, choral style, but also embellished and unembellished vocal solos, as well as instrumental falsobordoni (which were crucial to the evolution of the toccata).[27] Severi's ten *Salmi passaggiati* are embellished solo pieces with basso continuo. As with all vocal falsobordoni, they follow the shape of the ancient Gregorian psalm tones and are used for the singing of psalms. Severi's falsobordoni, like the psalm tones, are divided in half with each half consisting in its turn of a simple "recitation" over one chord and an embellished "cadence"; but in Severi's solo embellished compositions, as in similar works by Conforti and Bovicelli, the embellishment is highly virtuoso in style and, thus, far removed from the classical falsobordone.[28] Severi even occasionally embellished the recitation as well as the cadence.[29]

Severi also retained the old psalm tone melodies, presenting them in simple fashion in the first verse of each setting; he labeled this first verse "intonatione," perhaps because it uses the psalm tone intonation. The remaining verses, labeled "falsobordoni," are brilliant solo vocal embellishments of this opening verse. In these "falsobordoni," the psalm tone *cantus firmus* is either elaborated on in the vocal part or implied in the basso continuo harmonies. The lack of a "real" *cantus firmus* has an exact parallel in the Venetian keyboard toccatas that developed out of keyboard falsobordoni, which in their turn were elaborations of simpler choral pieces; so, too, Severi developed his "falsobordoni" out of simpler "intonationi."[30] Actually all the verses set by Severi are falsobordoni, since each has the recitation-cadence form; but by calling his first verse an "intonatione," the composer drew a clear distinction between the simple style of the first verse and the elaborations or variations in the verses that follow.

Indeed, the embellished falsobordoni by Severi are variations. In all verses the organ bass stays the same, but "each voice . . . , whether soprano, contralto, tenor, or bass, varied the melody and made it more artful."[31] The variations maintain the harmonies of the "intonatione" or first verse, although they begin with the recitation harmony. For instance, in no. [2], *Confitebor*, the embellished verses begin with a B-flat triad for the recitation; in the first verse or "intonatione"

this B-flat triad does not appear until m. 4, after the chant intonation. In no. [1], *Dixit Dominus*, a D triad is used for the recitation instead of the F harmony of the first verse (cf. mm. 5, 23, 37, 53, 70, and 86). Psalm tone V proved to be especially troublesome to composers of the sixteenth century, because it ends on an A and not on the modal final, F, and it has a B-natural in the melody. In his setting of psalm tone V (no. [5], *Laudate Dominum*), Severi changed the harmonies drastically from the "pure" setting of the psalm tone in the simple "intonatione" to the free settings in the embellished "falsobordoni." Tone VII also presented problems, and Severi transposed it down a fifth (see no. [7], *Nisi Dominus*).[32]

In his pieces, Severi used the letter *t* (for *trillo*) in two ways.[33] Most often, he placed the trill between two repeated notes when both are unaccented and usually dissonant passing notes with generally short rhythmic values (see the example on p. x). Only now and then did he put a trill between notes of different pitches or on accented notes. Severi's *trillo* is a *tremolo* or vibrato, and not the "ugly and awkward series of newly articulated repeated notes perpetrated by so many twentieth-century singers."[34]

Severi's written-out embellishments are of two kinds: there are those that revolve around one note, and those that are more expansive, involving scale passages or sequentially treated motivic ideas. The example on p. x from the setting of psalm tone II (*Confitebor*) shows both types of *passaggi*. (Brackets mark off different embellishments; the number 1 refers to *passaggi* that embellish a single note, 2a refers to sequential passages, and 2b refers to scale passages. Two instances of the *trillo*, or modern *tremolo* (*t*), occur in the second measure of the example.) Their frequent outlining of triads indicates that Severi's embellishments are often harmonically inspired. The "F" indication in m. 32 of the example is discussed below in the section Notes on Performance.

Each falsobordone shows a judicious balance between these two kinds of *passaggi*. Most often Severi started and ended his embellished sections by decorating a single note. Surrounded by these simpler elaborations are the more adventurous *passaggi*. He usually saved the most brilliant elaborations for the later verses of a piece (although the subdued "Gloria" of no. [3] is an exception), and he emphasized this build-up of embellishments by changes of meter, by dynamic contrasts, or, in nos. [9] and [10], by an increase in the number of parts being embellished. Severi's music reveals the delight that early seventeenth-century composers took in elaborating single musical ideas. Repeated motives abound, as do sequences, and both of these techniques fit in with Severi's goal of writing "embellishments that are as far as possible uniform."

Remarkable as it seems, the long strings of rapidly

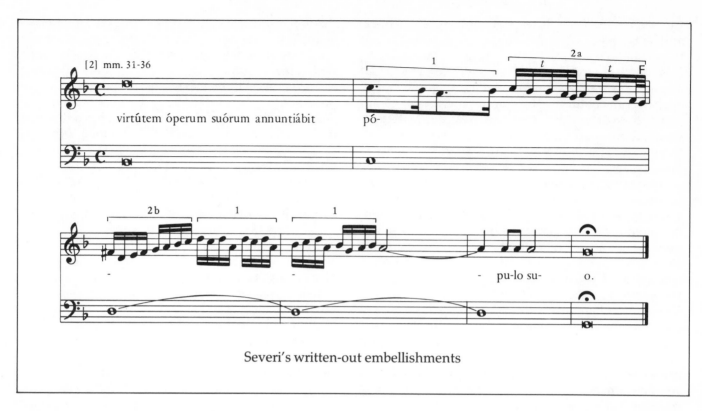

Severi's written-out embellishments

executed notes, the scale passages of two octaves, and the leaps of diminished fifths, augmented fourths, and even two octaves were, in Severi's mind, only of moderate difficulty. Although, as Severi wrote, "some . . . attempt difficult and inordinate embellishments," this was not his intent. His falsobordoni but "conform to the ecclesiastical style of Rome," and can be sung by "a good as well as a mediocre talent."

However, Severi's embellishments are just as complex as those found in Donatiello Coya's 1622 setting of Dentice's *Miserere*.[35] Dentice's *Miserere* (see Appendices A and B) and Severi's and Coya's settings of it (no. [10] and Appendix C, respectively) are presented in this edition for the sake of comparison. Dentice's *Miserere* is important because it is the first *Miserere* composition we know of to be notated with written-out embellishments, first in the setting by Severi in 1615, and later in the setting by Coya. Dentice's work stands at the very beginning of a long line of compositions whose embellished performance spans almost 300 years.[36] The two settings by Severi and Coya also show how two different composers embellished the same piece. Coya treated the falsobordone form in a looser way than did Severi, and he favored embellishments that are more flowing and that have a less rigid use of repetitive figures and dotted rhythms. He was also fond of frequent entrances after short rests.

Giovanni Luca Conforti, in his *Salmi passaggiati*, printed between 1601 and 1603 (the soprano settings were reprinted in 1607 and 1618), favored steady rhythmical values, just as Severi did. Even when Conforti used dotted figures, he did so only for a short time

and without Severi's rigidity. Conforti's publications were clearly a model for Severi's psalms of 1615: the collections of both Conforti and Severi are devoted entirely to embellished falsobordoni; these collections were both written by members of the Sistine Chapel; both have, to a certain extent, a teaching purpose; both use the ornament sign *t* for *trillo* (although Conforti also uses *g* for *groppo*); and both are intended for direct use in the liturgy.[37]

Notes on Performance

In his introduction to the *Salmi passaggiati* (see p. xxii), Severi gave some rules of performance that apply not only to his own music, but to early baroque music in general. In his first, second, and fifth rules, Severi emphasized sweet and graceful singing. According to Severi, the correct way to do this is to sing "not from the throat," with muscular action, but "from the chest," with correct breathing. Severi stressed the same vocal elements (sweetness, gracefulness, and firmness of tone) that are expressed by many other sixteenth- and seventeenth-century writers.[38]

When he wrote in rule one that "the intonation [should] be sung *adagio*," Severi showed that he was working with a rhythm based not on a steady *tactus*, but, rather, on a beat that varies according to different tempos. Until 1600, the *tactus* had dominated art music: the *tactus* was a time span, a simple duration, that was steady and absolute. The time span of the new "beat," on the other hand, was not absolute, but changed according to the different tempos used.

x

Severi's slow "intonationi" and faster "falsobordoni" have the same mensuration signs, the same apparent *tactus*; but the tempo and beat of each are different.[39]

Moreover, with Severi's music, we are on the threshold of modern notation: his note shapes approximate the modern ones; time signs like $\frac{12}{8}$ occur along with the ubiquitous C; dynamic marks are occasionally given (e.g., *forte* and *piano* in nos. [6], [7], and [8]); and the smallest of note values are used.[40]

Severi did not want a strict rhythm maintained during the embellishments. He wrote, "The singer should stop when he comes across the letter F [for *fermare* or *fermata*]." The reason Severi suggested this is to avoid the singing of "one *passaggio* right after another." A *passaggio* is an embellishing pattern, melodic and rhythmic, that is kept up for some time and then gives way either to another pattern or to a note of length. The *fermata* as expressed by the "F"-sign is, in effect, a retard, or slowing up of the musical motion; these signs are "musical punctuation marks showing the listener that something new is about to happen."[41]

Moreover, Severi did not want a strict rhythm maintained during the recitations, since, in general, he advised the singers to hold a first syllable, "passing over the second one quickly, and so on with every two syllables." He wrote, "Take care to hold the last syllable of a word." Since in one of the places where Severi did write out the recitation (see no. [10], mm. 70-72) he treated his own rules freely, the point seems to be that recitations are sung in a free, rhetorical rhythm, with first and last syllables and every other syllable within a word being held longer than other syllables.

Two of Severi's rules concern dotted rhythms. His third rule is that "when *crome* [= eighth-notes] are sung that have a dot on the first one, they [the dotted *crome*] are sung in a lively way, but not too quickly, and the dots are not emphasized too much." In rule four Severi said that "when there are *crome* that have a dot on the second one, they are not sung too quickly," and "to gain ease in singing, it will be necessary to pass quickly over the first *croma* and hold the second one."

Severi, then, is one of the first to mention explicitly the baroque practice of holding a dotted eighth a bit longer and speeding up the following sixteenth-note, or, in the case of a sixteenth followed by a dotted eighth, the "Lombard rhythm," of "passing quickly over the first *croma* and holding the second one." Both dotted rhythms occur frequently in Severi's music.[42] Also, his comment that "the dots are not emphasized too much" implies a clear distinction between ♪ and ♫. A dotted note indicates some sort of vocal emphasis on the dot itself, and not a mere holding over of the sound.

Two others of Severi's rules concern text treatment and the use of *musica ficta*. In the seventh rule, Severi wrote that "when notes have a *virgola*, ↓ one should sing a syllable on that note." Most often he used the *virgola* (see [no. 2], m. 43) when a syllable-change comes on an unexpected rhythmic value, such as on the last sixteenth-note of a measure; its sole purpose is to ensure clarity of text treatment. Word-painting is infrequent, and the setting of the word "occasum" (downfall) in no. [4], mm. 17-20, where the bass "falls" or "sinks" two octaves, is a striking exception to Severi's usual style. Text-accents are almost always correct in the source print, although exceptions do occur (as at no. [1], mm. 44-50; no. [3], mm. 42-45; and no. [10], mm. 53-55). With regard to *musica ficta*, Severi said that it is absolutely essential to use it because "by observing this, one at least will not destroy the true falsobordoni of Rome."

In his ninth rule Severi wrote that he had tried to make his embellishments "seem natural and improvised." Indeed, said Severi, "similar embellishments are customarily improvised by good singers, both in Rome and elsewhere." Improvisation was not only enormously important at the time; it was actually preferred over written music. Vicentino, for instance, wrote in 1555 that "when music is sung 'alla mente,' it is more pleasing than when it is sung from the written page. To take an example from preaching and oratory, a sermon and talk read from the written page have no grace, nor do they please the audience."[43]

Although Severi made no comment on tempo, aside from saying that "intonationi" should be sung *adagio*, a satisfactory *tempo giusto* in modern terms is ♩ = M.M. 85. Curt Sachs pointed out that in 1619 Praetorius "fixed the tempo at 'a good moderate speed': 160 *tempora* should be played in a quarter of an hour."[44] This is a good tempo for Severi's *Salmi*, also. In Severi's day, music was freely sung at different pitches,[45] and his pieces can be transposed. However, because of the virtuoso style and the large range of individual parts, especially the bass line, the level of transposition is limited:

Vocal ranges in Severi's *Salmi passaggiati*

Severi wrote these solo falsobordoni for soprano, alto, tenor, and bass soloists. The usual quartet of voices was not, as today, two male and two female voices; but the alto, tenor, and bass music was usually sung by male voices. Moreover, soprano parts were sung by boys, falsettos, or *castrati*. Matteo Fornari, a singer in the Papal Chapel, wrote in his *Narrazione istorica* of 1749, that "in the countries of France, Spain, and Germany, young boys for the most part sang the soprano parts, but among them were always some falsettos." Fornari added that in Rome boys also sang in basilicas and other churches. However, Hucke tells us that in the Sistine, soprano parts were sung by falsettos until around 1600, when *castrati* began to supersede them: "the use of *castrati* sopranos began in 1588 in the person of Giacomo Spagnoletto, whom Agostino Martini in his *Diario* labeled a *Eunnuco*." Alto voices in the Sistine "were unquestionably always natural voices," but alto *castrati* did sing "in other churches and in theatres" and, in later years, even in the Sistine.[46]

Severi most likely intended his psalm settings to be accompanied by the organ, although other instruments can be used. According to their title pages, Conforti's embellished falsobordoni published between 1601 and 1603, for instance, have "the bass placed underneath, suitable for playing and singing with the organ or other instruments," and in 1623, Heinrich Schütz preferred four "violen di gamba" to accompany the narrator's lines or, as the composer called them, the falsobordoni. If these instruments were unavailable, Schütz said that an organ or some other instrument, like a lute or pandora, might be used.[47]

Severi attached no name at all to the instrumental accompaniment. He notated only a few figures and accidentals, even though more of them could well have been used.[48] Furthermore, the bass line is made up of sustained breves that change every measure, and there is no indication as to whether the chord position is to change over these long notes or not. Unlike Viadana, who put the accompaniment to his *Cento concertí ecclesiastici* (1602) into a separate partbook, Severi placed his accompaniment directly below the voice lines, so that the accompanist is never in doubt as to what is happening above his part.

Because of the virtuoso brilliance of these vocal lines, the continuo part should be simple. However, during recitations embellishments must be added by the accompanist, even though they were not written out by the composer. Heinrich Schütz, in the preface

to his *Auferstehungshistorie* of 1623, wrote that during the falsobordoni, that is, during the narrator's recitation on one note, "it is the organist whose person comes to the fore." As long as the recitation lasts, the accompanist should play, "always elegantly and appropriately, runs or *passaggi* . . . which will give to this work, as well as all other falsobordoni, the correct style." Schütz's comment is not an idle suggestion, but a firm rule, established to attain "the correct style" of falsobordone performance.[49]

A clue to the kind of embellishment Schütz had in mind is found in Conforti's *Salmi passaggiati* of 1603. Unlike Severi, Conforti did embellish the recitations of his psalms, and this vocal style is probably very much like the keyboard style demanded by Schütz. In the following examples of possible (editorial) accompaniments to two of Severi's recitation settings, the keyboard part is stylistically derived from Conforti's recitation embellishments. The vocal rhythm of Severi's recitation is also supplied editorially in these examples. Both keyboard embellishments and vocal declamations show a style at which performers might aim.

Severi's pieces are "to be sung at Sunday Vespers and feast days throughout the year."[50] Usually he set only the odd-numbered verses and the complete minor doxology (*Gloria Patri*) of each psalm, leaving even-numbered verses to be performed in other ways. There are only three exceptions to this general practice: he set all the verses of no. [5], *Laudate Dominum*, because it is quite short; on the other hand, he set only part of no. [9], *In exitu*, and no. [10], *Miserere*, because of their great length. The important *Caeremoniale episcoporum* of 1600 states that the entire minor doxology (the *Gloria Patri* and the *Sicut erat*) must always be sung "by the choir in a loud voice" and must not be supplanted by the organ verses.[51] The remaining verses in Severi's psalms, however, can be performed in Gregorian chant, or as choral falsobordoni or instrumental versets.[52]

The instrumental versets, in their turn, can be done

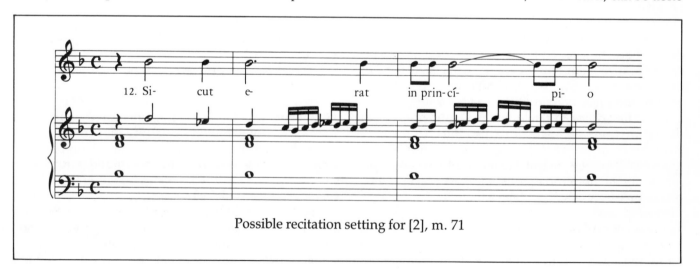

Possible recitation setting for [2], m. 71

Possible recitation setting for [6], m. 13

in two ways. The *Caeremoniale episcoporum* suggests that if they *substitute* for sung verses, either "someone in the choir should recite in a loud voice what is not sung because of the playing of the organ," or else someone should "sing the same [text] in a clear voice along with the organ."[53] In the latter case, the organist must stay close to the melodies or implied harmonies of the *cantus firmus* because, along with his paraphrase, a singer will be adding some sort of melody.[54] A second way of performing the psalm texts, found in Bottazzi's *Choro et organo* of 1614, is to sing all the verses but also to insert an instrumental verset after every other sung verse.[55]

Regardless of what *alternatim* practice is used, the instrumentalist must create a paraphrase of the falsobordone. Several instrumental falsobordoni (almost all are for keyboard) have come down to us and serve as examples for the keyboard performer. They range in style from simple vocal copies to elaborate embellishments of the choral falsobordone. Indeed, the more brilliant paraphrases, with their block chords and sweeping figurations, are historically important, since it is from such pieces that the keyboard intonation and toccata evolved.[56]

If an organ is used for versets or for the basso continuo, the sound should not be an overwhelming one.

The distinctive quality of the Italian organ at this time was light and silvery, "lively and sweet at the same time."[57] Typically, this organ had one manual with soft, delicate principals (from 8' to 1') and flutes (4' to 2') and a modest pedal board. Antegnati explicitly advised the organist to change the registration often in playing, since "the world is beautiful because of its variety, and there is no beautiful thing that if continued too long does not become tedious."[58]

The Edition

The following libraries have copies of Severi's *Salmi passaggiati*, published by Niccolò Borboni in 1615: Brussels, Bibliothèque Royale Albert I;[59] Florence, Conservatorio Musicale, B. 3813 and B. 2561; London, The British Library, K. 3. f. 8; London, Royal College of Music, RCM II, B. 11; Milan, Conservatorio di Musica "G. Verdi"; Paris, Bibliothèque nationale; and Rome, Conservatorio di Musica "S. Cecilia." Copies of Severi's *Salmi passaggiati* are no longer held by either the Deutsche Staatsbibliothek, Berlin, or the Bayerische Staatsbibliothek, Munich.[60]

Borboni's 1615 publication of Severi's pieces is very small, measuring about 5½ inches in length and 3½ inches in height (about 14 cm. × 9 cm.). It is not just a self-effacing statement, then, when Severi spoke of his work as a "libretto" or "little book." As with most of Borboni's publications, the volume is attractive and has very few printing errors. Engraved in copper throughout and in oblong format, there are seventy-five pages of music, numbered consecutively, together with three pages of introductory material—a single dedicatory page and two pages "ai lettori"—and a concluding *tavola*, or table of contents.

In the present edition, the following editorial changes have been made: (1) Modern clefs replace the original C-clefs (which are given in the incipits). (2) Ligatures are indicated by brackets; broken brackets are used to indicate coloration, which is rare. (3) Redundant accidentals are eliminated (but listed in the Critical Notes), and the older sharp sign is changed to a natural sign when necessary. (4) *Musica ficta* is indicated above the vocal staff and is valid for an entire measure; in the accompaniment, *musica ficta* is added in brackets on the staff. (5) Barring is made uniform and regular (Severi omitted barlines at the ends of lines and after penultimate cadence measures). (6) Figured bass numbers are placed under the staff (Severi sometimes put them above the bass line); the realization is by the editor, but the performer is to add embellishments during recitations.[61] (7) Chant verses are added (in italic type at the end of each piece) for an *alternatim* performance; although not found in the original, these verses were more than likely used in performance. (8) Page numbers from the original publication are cited in the Critical Notes; psalm verses and measure numbers are added on the music pages of this edition. (9) Psalm-texts are modernized, and punctuation and spelling are taken from the *Liber Usualis*. (10) Round breves (◐) are used here in place of Severi's longs (ꟼ) during the recitations: these notes are of an indeterminate value, lasting as long as the recitation of the text demands. (11) Double bars are inserted after all mediant and final cadences. (12) Accents are added for words of more than two syllables (two-syllable words are invariably accented on penultimate syllables).

By and large, there was no need to change time signatures or reduce note values (a semibreve in the source is transcribed here as a whole-note). The original texts of the psalms Severi set have been modernized here, since the differences between the originals and their modern equivalents (as they appear in the 1950 edition of the *Liber Usualis*) are minor—such differences include various forms of "s" and the use of "u" for "v," or "e" for "ae," as well as variations in spacing, capitalization, punctuation, abbreviations (usually the omission of an "n" or "m" indicated by a dash), use of accent marks, and spelling. Unless a striking change occurs, these differences are not listed in the Critical Notes.

Critical Notes

The Critical Notes include the following information: the location (in parentheses) of the piece in Severi's original publication of 1615; the psalm and psalm tone number of each work, together with its liturgical use (and with its location in the 1950 edition of the *Liber Usualis*); modern editions of any piece (with fuller bibliographical information reserved for the Selected Bibliography); and a description of the original source music when any alteration was made in the present edition. Pitch references are based on the Helmholtz system of pitch designation (e.g., c′ stands for middle c).

[1] Dixit Dominus (pp. 1-7)

Psalm 109 [Psalm Tone I].
First Psalm, Sunday Vespers; *Liber Usualis*, pp. 128, 251-252.
Modern edition: Goldschmidt, *Die italienische Gesangsmethode* (Breslau, 1890), pp. 48-49, prints mm. 53-69.
Alternate verses in chant added by the editor. M. 11, all parts, note 1 is a breve (double whole-note). M. 41, notated sharp-signs on beats 2 and 3. M. 67, solo, note 1 is an eighth-note tied to a sixteenth-note. M. 89, solo, note 1 is an eighth-note. M. 99, solo, final note has a sharp-sign.

[2] Confitebor tibi Domine (pp. 8-14)

Psalm 110 [Psalm Tone II, transposed up a fourth].
Second Psalm, Sunday Vespers; *Liber Usualis*, pp. 134-135, 252.
Alternate verses in chant added by the editor. Mm. 21 and 45, solo, notated sharp-sign on the second f′ in each measure. M. 64, all parts, time signature is $\frac{8}{12}$.

[3] Beatus vir (pp. 15-21)

Psalm 111 [Psalm Tone III].
Third Psalm, Sunday Vespers; *Liber Usualis*, pp. 142-143, 253.
Alternate verses in chant added by the editor. M. 13, solo, notes 9, 13, and 15 have notated flats. Mm. 15-16, bass, figures placed above the bass line. M. 32, solo, note 3 has a notated sharp. M. 48, solo, note 6 has a notated flat. M. 76, solo, note 8 has a notated sharp.

[4] Laudate pueri (pp. 22-28)

Psalm 112 [Psalm Tone IV].
Fourth Psalm, Sunday Vespers; *Liber Usualis*, pp. 150, 254.
Alternate verses in chant added by the editor. M. 13, solo, note 3 has a notated sharp. M. 16, solo, note 8 has a notated sharp. M. 38, solo, notes 9, 13, and 16 have notated sharps. M. 39, solo, note 3 has a notated

sharp. M. 48, solo, note 4 has a notated sharp. M. 51, solo, final note has a notated sharp. M. 59, all parts, time signature is $\frac{8}{12}$. M. 79, all parts, time signature is $\frac{24}{16}$. M.80, all parts, time signature is $\frac{16}{24}$. M. 81, solo, final note has a notated sharp.

[5] Laudate Dominum (pp. 29-32)

Psalm 116 [Psalm Tone V].

Vesper Psalm; *Liber Usualis*, p. 168.

Mm. 11-12, bass, figures placed above the bass line. M. 13, all parts, key signature of one flat given in this measure and remains in effect until the end of the piece. M. 44, note 5 has a notated sharp (standing for a natural-sign). M. 45, solo, final note has a notated sharp.

[6] Magnificat (pp. 33-40)

Canticle of the Virgin (Luke 1) [Psalm Tone VI].

Closing of Vespers; *Liber Usualis*, pp. 211, 260.

Modern editions: Kuhn, *Die Verzierungs-Kunst* (Leipzig, 1902), pp. 142-145, prints the entire piece; Beyschlag, *Die Ornamentik der Musik* (Leipzig, 1908), p. 45, prints mm. 77-92; Fellerer, *The Monody* (Cologne, 1968), pp. 57-58, prints mm. 52-70; Goldschmidt, *Die Lehre von der vokalen Ornamentik* (Charlottenburg, 1907), pp. 3 and 5, prints mm. 78-80; and Goldschmidt, *Die italienische Gesangsmethode* (Breslau, 1890), p. 48, prints mm. 77-91. Severi used a chant intonation only for the first verse; alternate verses added by the editor then make use of the regular sixth mode psalm tone without intonation.

M. 34, solo, note 1 is a quarter-note.

[7] Nisi Dominus (pp. 41-46)

Psalm 126 [Psalm Tone VII, transposed down a fifth].

Vesper Psalm; *Liber Usualis*, pp. 176-177.

Alternate chant verses added by the editor. M. 48, solo, notes 2 and 3 replaced by a dotted quarter-note (c').

[8] In convertendo (pp. 47-53)

Psalm 125 [Psalm Tone VIII].

Vesper Psalm; *Liber Usualis*, p. 175.

Alternate chant verses added by the editor. M. 13, all parts, from here to the end Severi used a partial signature, namely a flat in the voice line for the first half of each verse; in verse 7 the instrumental part also has a flat in the first half of the verse. Mm. 19-23, solo, the *Liber Usualis* text is "cum eis" rather than "nobiscum." M. 35, solo, final note has a notated sharp. M. 35, last note-m. 36, solo, these 2 notes are slurred together (for text reasons). M. 38, solo, last 2 notes in the measure are sixteenth-notes. M. 72, solo, final note has a notated sharp.

[9] In exitu (pp. 54-66)

Psalm 113 [Psalm Tone *Tonus Peregrinus* or *Misto Tuono*].

Last Psalm, Sunday Vespers; *Liber Usualis*, pp. 160-161.

Modern editions: Beyschlag, *Die Ornamentik der Musik* (Leipzig, 1908), p. 46, prints mm. 136-149; Bradshaw, *The Falsobordone* (Neuhausen-Stuttgart, 1978), p. 108, prints mm. 143-149.

Alternate chant verses added by the editor. M. 11, all parts, note 1 is a breve (double whole-note). M. 17, bass, occupied by a breve (double whole-note). Mm. 34 and 49, bass is lacking. M. 85, solo, note 6 has a notated sharp. M. 100, solo, final note has a notated sharp. M. 122, solo, final note has a notated sharp. M. 133, solo, note 8 has a notated sharp. M. 148, solo, final note has a notated sharp.

[10] Miserere (pp. 67-75)

Psalm 50 [based on Fabrizio Dentice's setting of this text].

Matins and Lauds of Holy Week, *Tenebrae* service; *Liber Usualis*, p. 734.

Modern edition: Beyschlag, *Die Ornamentik der Musik*, p. 47, prints mm. 87-95.

Alternate chant verses added by the editor to psalm tone IV. The five-part setting by Dentice used as the basis for this piece is transcribed in Appendix B (p. 72 below); Appendix A (p. 71) is an earlier version. M. 7, solo, note 6 has a notated sharp. M. 36, solo, final note has a notated sharp. M. 48, solo, notes 13 and 14 are thirty-second-notes; final note has a notated sharp. M. 48, final note-m. 49, note 1, solo, these 2 notes are slurred together. M. 55, solo, final note has a notated sharp. M. 59, solo, note 2 consists of 2 tied sixteenth-notes (a, a). M. 85, solo, final note has a notated sharp. M. 85, final note-m. 86, note 1, solo, these 2 notes are slurred together.

Appendix A. Dentice, *Miserere* (p. 29)

Lamentationi di Fabricio Dentice . . . M. D. LXXXXIII (RISM D 1659), p. 29.

Dentice's volume contains seven falsobordone settings of the *Miserere*, of which this is the last. It is without text. This is the original form of the work given in Appendix B. The *Urform* is for four voices, is written a fourth higher, is without text, and has a different final cadence from the one Severi used. M. 7, all parts, last note is a long.

Appendix B. Dentice, *Miserere*

MS Cappella Sistina 205 (ca. 1630) (Bradshaw, *The Falsobordone*, p. 186, no. 136*).

The piece is found twice in the codex, on folios 5v-8r and 40v-43r. Both times it is the *primus chorus* (MS Cappella Sistina 205) of a double choir work, the second chorus of which (MS Cappella Sistina 206) has different music and is attributed first to Dentice and, in later folios, to "Domini Nanini." The scribe notated verses 5, 9, 13, and 17 (with verses 3, 7, 11, 15, and 19 reserved for the second choir). Only the first verse is given here.

Appendix C. Dentice-Coya, *Miserere* (pp. 15 and 18)

Responsorii . . . di D. Gio. Domenica Viola . . . 1622, pp. 15-18 (Bradshaw, *The Falsobordone*, p. 181, no. 112*).

This is an embellished setting by Donatiello Coya of several verses of Dentice's *Miserere*. Recitation notes are all unmeasured longs (replaced here by unmeasured breves). In the source, verse 7 (p. 15) comes before verse 3 (p. 18). Mm. 1-11, only the bass is given, with the text placed beneath it. M. 24, solo, rest is an eighth-rest. Mm. 27 and 42, all parts, there is no apparent difference between C and ₵. M. 31, solo, final note has a notated sharp. M. 44, solo, note 13 is a sixteenth-note. M. 46, solo, final note has a notated sharp. M. 51, solo, final note has a notated sharp. M. 52, solo, final note is a quarter-note.

Acknowledgments

It pleases me greatly to thank all those who helped in preparing this edition of Severi's *Salmi passaggiati*. First of all, I wish to express my gratitude to the directors of European libraries who willingly sent along films and information on Severi's *Salmi*. These include François Lesure of the Bibliothèque nationale, Paris; Joan Littlejohn, Deputy Keeper of the Parry Room Library, Royal College of Music, London; Dr. R. Münster of the Bayerische Staatsbibliothek, Munich; O. W. Neighbour, Music Librarian, The British Library, London; Jutta Theurich, Librarian at the Deutsche Staatsbibliothek, Berlin; Prof. Emilia Zanetti, head of the Music Library of the Conservatorio di Musica, S. Cecilia, Rome; and the Music Librarian of the Bibliothèque Royale Albert I, Brussels.

I thank Professor Frederick F. Hammond for information on the Borghese coat of arms that adorns the title page of Severi's volume.

Frank Shelton and Robynn Bosler, my research assistants at the University of California, Los Angeles, were a continual help.

I thank, too, the Academic Research Committee of the University for several grants that aided in preparing this work.

Further, I am happy to thank the editorial staff of A-R Editions, Inc., whose care and circumspection in preparing this volume for publication were models of editorial integrity.

I finally wish to thank my wife, Doris, to whom my effort in this volume is dedicated.

Murray C. Bradshaw
July 1981   University of California, Los Angeles

Notes

1. Giuseppe Baini, *Memorie Storico-Critiche della Vita e delle Opere di Giovanni . . . da Palestrina*, I (Rome, 1828; repr. Hildesheim, 1966): 260, n. 356. Adami da Bolsena, a member of the Sistine Choir, noted that Severi "composed many falsobordoni on all the psalm tones, which, in 1615 he published and dedicated to Cardinal Borghese"; see *Osservazioni per ben regolare il coro dei cantori della cappella pontificia* (Rome, 1711), p. 194. On the falsobordoni, see Murray C. Bradshaw, *The Falsobordone, A Study in Renaissance and Baroque Music* (Neuhausen-Stuttgart, 1978).

2. This and all subsequent quotations of Severi that appear in this preface are from the introductory material to the 1615 publication of his *Salmi*; see pp. xx and xxii.

3. For a recent list of treatises on embellishment, see Howard M. Brown, *Embellishing 16th-Century Music* (London, 1976), pp. x-xi; see, too, Max Kuhn, *Die Verzierungs-Kunst* (Leipzig, 1902), Hugo Goldschmidt, *Die Lehre von der vokalen Ornamentik* (Charlottenburg, 1907), and Adolf Beyschlag, *Die Ornamentik der Musik* (Leipzig, 1908).

4. Severi is always described in his own publications, and in the writing of others, as a "Perugian."

5. Catalano, born in Enna, Sicily, around 1560, was not only *maestro di cappella* at S. Apollinare from 1603 to 1608 and from 1611 to 1613, but also held overlapping positions in the Oratorio of S. Marcello from 1606 to 1623, and with Marc'Antonio Borghese, the Prince of Sulmona, from 1611 to 1619. Catalano later returned to Sicily, where he died in 1644 or later. It was the close connection with the Borghese family that brought Severi and Catalano, student and teacher, together. Catalano's main publication, issued in 1616, was a volume of *Sacrarum cantionum* (Rome, 1616; RISM C 1520), although other works appeared in collections of his day. For new information on Catalano, see Thomas Culley, "A Documentary History of the Liturgical Music at the German College in Rome: 1573-1674" (Ph.D. diss., Harvard University, 1965), pp. 119-128 and 177-178.

6. See the title page (reproduced in this edition as Plate I). Borboni spent most of his life in Rome, where "he was well-known as organist, . . . engraver and composer"; see Nigel Fortune, "Italian Secular Song from 1600 to 1630: The Origins and Development of Accompanied Monody" (Ph.D. diss., Cambridge University, 1953), Appendix 3, p. 68, and Claudio Sartori, *Dizionario degli editori musicali italiani* (Florence, 1958), pp. 31-32. Borboni was also the publisher of Frescobaldi's music.

7. Scipione Borghese was the Pope's nephew, the son of the Pontiff's sister (he later changed his name from Caffarelli to Borghese). He became Papal Secretary of State in 1605, and was extremely wealthy and influential. Like most members of the

Borghese family, he was a generous patron of the arts. Marc'Antonio Borghese, for whom Catalano worked, was another nephew of Paul V, the son of the Pope's younger brother. In 1612, Mocenigo, the Venetian ambassador, said that "while his Holiness loaded Cardinal Borghese with ecclesiastical offices and revenues, he heaped secular benefits upon Marc'Antonio, who already bore the title of Prince of Sulmona"; Ludwig von Pastor, *The History of the Popes*, XXVI, trans. E. Graf (St. Louis, 1937): 54-55, 61, 63-68 passim.

8. A. Celani, "I cantori della Cappella Pontificia nei secoli XVI-XVIII," *Rivista Musicale Italiana* XIV (1907): 772. See also Franz Xaver Haberl, "Das traditionelle Musikprogramm der sixtinischen Kapelle nach den Aufzeichnungen von Andrea Adami da Bolsena," *Kirchenmusikalisches Jahrbuch* XII (1897): 55.

9. Herman-Walther Frey, "Die Gesänge der Sixtinischen Kapelle an den Sonntagen und Hohen Kirchenfesten des Jahres 1616," *Mélanges Eugène Tisserant* VI (Vatican City, 1964): 404, 413-414, 422, 425-429.

10. See Remo Giazotto, *Quattro secoli di storia dell'Accademia Nazionale di Santa Cecilia* (Rome, 1970), I: 102; Giazotto also included facsimiles of the dedication and first page of the "ai lettori" of Severi's *Salmi passaggiati*, on p. 103.

11. Josephus M. Llorens, *Capellae Sixtinae Codices* (Vatican City, 1960), pp. 53 and 145-146; Franz Xaver Haberl, *Bibliographischer und thematischer Musikkatalog* (Leipzig, 1888), p. 32.

12. See Vogel, *Bibliografia della musica italiana vocale profana pubblicata dal 1500 al 1700* (Hildesheim, 1972), II: 211; see, too, the revised edition of Vogel's *Bibliographia* (1977), pp. 1622-1624. Vogel noted that the only copy of Severi's *Arie* was in Oscar Chilesotti's private library. Chilesotti wrote an article on the volume and printed eight pieces from it; see "Canzonette del Seicento con la Chitarra," *Rivista Musicale Italiana* XVI (1909): 847-862. Jan Racek analyzed brief sections of the *Arie* in *Stilprobleme der italienischen Monodie* (Prague, 1965), pp. 143-145. In his *Musikalisches Lexicon* of 1732, J. G. Walther mentioned only Severi's *Arie* of 1626 and not the *Salmi*; see facs. ed. (Kassel, 1953), p. 567.

13. Celani, "I cantori," p. 772. Remo Giazotto discussed the entire "clamorous incident," as he called it, in his *Quattro secoli*, I: 93-109; Giazotto also included Pope Urban VIII's original brief setting up the "congregatione" in 1624 (pp. 93-96), two letters from the Sistine Choir singers protesting abuses of the "congregatione" (pp. 99, 101), the notice in the Sistine *Diario* of the actions taken against Severi by the "congregatione" (p. 104), and, finally, Urban's rectification of those abuses (pp. 105-108).

14. Allegri, Giovannelli, and Landi were members of the Sistine; other composers represented included Severi's teacher, Catalano, as well as Boschetti, Costantini, Quagliati, Tarditi, Ugolini, Zoili, and the famous organist Frescobaldi.

15. G. L. P. Sievers, "Die päpstliche Kapelle zu Rom," *Allgemeine Musikalische Zeitung* XXIV (1825): 378.

16. Celani, "I cantori," p. 772.

17. Baini, *Memorie Storico-Critiche*, II: 31, n. 469.

18. Celani, "I cantori," p. 780.

19. Celani, "I cantori," p. 772. Severi's tomb is apparently no longer at S. Maria Odigitria, but many of the tombs in this church were covered over when it was rebuilt in 1804, and Severi's may well have been one of them. *Grove's Dictionary* (5th ed.) says that Severi was buried at S. Maria in Aracoeli, but I have been unable to locate the tomb in this church. I thank Sister Francis Hailer, RSHM of the Curia Generalizia, Istituto del Sacro Cuore di Maria, Rome, for this information.

20. Baini, *Memorie Storico-Critiche*, II: 31-32, n. 469.

21. Ludwig von Pastor, *The History of the Popes*, XXVI: 460.

22. Ibid., XXIX: 543-544. Urban VIII commissioned Bernini to build the famous baldacchino over the main altar of St. Peter's basilica. Urban also built the Palazzo Barberini, the theater of which was inaugurated in 1634 by a performance of the sacred opera *Sant' Alessio*, with music by Stefano Landi and libretto by Cardinal Giulio Rospigliosi, later Clement IX.

23. The text of the *Miserere* is Psalm 50 or, in the Hebrew order, Psalm 51. Fabrizio Dentice was a renowned musician. Born ca. 1540, he was famous as a violist, lutanist, composer, and teacher. His early years were spent in Naples (he is often described as a "nobile cavaliere napolitano"). After some time in Rome, he entered the service of the duchy of Parma, where he died at least by 1601, well before Severi's embellished setting of his *Miserere*. Galilei (1581), Cerreto (1601), and d'India (1609) all speak highly of Dentice, and he is mentioned as early as 1561 in Maffei's *Delle Lettere*. Luigi Dentice, Fabrizio's father, wrote the *Due dialoghi* of 1552. Baini, *Memorie Storico-Critiche*, II: 195, n. 578, mistakenly attributed the *Miserere* of Fabrizio to Luigi. Scipione Dentice, a famous composer of madrigals (RISM D 1660, 1662-1667), is not Fabrizio's nephew, as is often claimed.

24. Ernst Ferand, "Didactic Embellishment Literature in the Late Renaissance" in *Aspects of Medieval and Renaissance Music* (New York, 1966), pp. 154-172, lists all the embellished compositions, treatises, and manuals, including, on p. 158, Severi's, written between 1535 and 1688.

25. Bradshaw, *The Falsobordone*, p. 21.

26. Ibid., p. 31.

27. For the evolution of falsobordone style and technique into those of the toccata, see Murray C. Bradshaw, *The Origin of the Toccata* ([Rome], 1972). The different kinds of sixteenth-century falsobordoni are discussed in Bradshaw, *The Falsobordone*, pp. 51-94.

28. The embellished falsobordoni by Conforti, Bovicelli, and others are discussed in Bradshaw, *The Falsobordone*, pp. 85-88 and 106-111. An edition and study of Conforti's *Salmi passaggiati* of 1601-1603 by this author will soon be published by the American Institute of Musicology.

29. Embellishment occurs during the recitations of the following pieces: [1], m. 92; [4], mm. 54-55 and 60-61; [10], mm. 38-40, 61-65, 70, and 78. Severi regularly linked recitation and cadence by a short embellished passage.

30. See Bradshaw, *The Origin of the Toccata*, pp. 19-40.

31. Baini, *Memorie Storico-Critiche*, I: 260, n. 356. See also Robert Haas, *Aufführungspraxis der Musik* (Potsdam, 1931), p. 113.

32. For a discussion of tonality in the falsobordone, ca. 1600, see Bradshaw, *The Falsobordone*, pp. 60-64 and 99-100. In the early seventeenth century, falsobordoni in tone V were almost always written in F major, exactly like Severi's "falsobordoni" in tone V (but not like his "intonatione").

33. Italian composers in general were reluctant, in the early baroque at least, to use symbols for embellishments. They preferred either to write embellishments out, as Severi most often did, or to improvise them *alla mente*.

34. Brown, *Embellishing 16th-Century Music*, p. 10, n. 3; also see Giulio Caccini, *Le Nuove Musiche*, ed. H. Wiley Hitchcock, Recent Researches in the Music of the Baroque, vol. IX (Madison, Wisconsin: A-R Editions, Inc., 1970), p. 51, n. 32.

35. Dentice's own falsobordone setting of the *Miserere* text first appeared in his *Lamentationi* of 1593 (RISM D 1659). Almost forty years later this setting was slightly changed and copied into the great Sistine collection of *Miserere* compositions, Capp. Sist. Cod. 205-206. Since Dentice's earlier version of 1593 is somewhat different from the later one in the Sistine codices (which is the one Severi and Coya embellished), both versions of Dentice's *Miserere* are given in Appendices A and B of this edition.

36. See Flavio Testi, *La musica italiana nel medioeva e nel rinascimento* (Milan, 1969), p. 501, and Julius Amann, *Allegris Miserere und die Aufführungspraxis in der Sixtina* (Regensburg,

1935). Giovanelli wrote a *Miserere* that also became famous in the early seventeenth century; see Frey, "Die Gesänge der Sixtinischen Kapelle," p. 412, n. 43.

37. See note 28.

38. In 1556, for instance, Heinrich Finck wrote that "one should sing pleasantly and tenderly," and added that no voice part should become so strained "that the singers lose their color, and become black in the face and run out of breath . . . and that the basses grumble as if they were locked in a barrel full of hornets or else puff like busted wind bellows"; see Raymund Schlecht, "Hermann Finck über die Kunst des Singens, 1556," *Monatshefte für Musikgeschichte* XI (1879): 136-137. Coclicus (1552), Viadana (1602), and Diruta (1609) are among the many who emphasized gracefulness and elegance in singing. William James Henderson said that Severi's comments mean "the end is to be reached by management of the breath and not by muscular action of the throat"; see Henderson, *Early History of Singing* (1921; repr. ed., New York, 1969), pp. 122-123.

39. See Harald Heckmann, "Der Takt in der Musiklehre des 17. Jahrhunderts," *Archiv für Musikwissenschaft* X (1953): 116. Imogene Horsley pointed out that improvised singing, with its fast embellishments, probably had a great deal to do with this change in rhythmic thought, "although none of the diminution treatises discuss the problem"; see "The Diminutions in Composition and Theory of Composition," *Acta Musicologica* XXXV (1963): 130, n. 23a.

40. H. Schmidl, in the *Dizionario universale dei musicisti* (Milan, 1929), s. v. "Severi," wrote that "Severi was among the first composers in whose works the *crome, semicrome, fuse,* and even the *trillo* are found."

41. Bradshaw, *The Falsobordone*, p. 110. For examples of *fermate* after one *passaggio* and before a note of length see no. [9], mm. 19-22, 28, 46, 58, 64, 75, 92-93, 104-105, 116, 121, 140, and 147. For examples of *fermate* between different *passaggi*, see no. [9], mm. 37, 44, 57, and 110. Severi did not consistently mark *fermate* in all cases where he might have done so (see measures 49-50 and 53 of no. [9]), and sometimes he marked them where we don't expect him to (see no. [9], mm. 69-70).

42. Beyschlag, in *Die Ornamentik der Musik*, 2nd ed., (Leipzig, 1953), p. 33, wrote that "we note especially the rhythmic figure 𝅘𝅥𝅮. 𝅘𝅥𝅮. , which appeared shortly after 1600, chiefly in the works of Severi, Marini, and others; a century later the same rhythm, called 'in the Lombard fashion,' would be considered something quite new." See also Goldschmidt, *Die italienische Gesangsmethode* (Breslau, 1890), p. 123.

43. Vicentino, *L'Antica musica ridotta alla moderna prattica* (Rome, 1555; repr. ed., 1959), IV: 42.

44. Curt Sachs, *Rhythm and Tempo* (New York, 1953), p. 203; Michael Praetorius, *Syntagma musicum* (Wolfenbüttel, 1619; facs. ed., Kassel, 1958), III: 88.

45. Transposition goes back at least to the early sixteenth century. In 1511, Arnolt Schlick wrote that "people sing higher in one place than in another because they have voices of small or large ranges," and an organist needs to know "what to do according to the voices of the choir"; *Spiegel der Orgelmacher und Organisten* (Heidelberg, 1511; mod. ed., Ernst Flade: Mainz, 1932), p. 15. Other theorists—for example, Bermudo (1555), Banchieri (1605), Agazzari (1607), Diruta (1609), and Praetorius (1619)—also commented on the use of transposition.

46. Hucke, "Die Besetzung von Sopran und Alt in der Sixtinischen Kapelle," *Miscelánea en homenaje a Monseñor Higinio Anglés* (Barcelona, 1958-61), I: 382-393. The last falsetto in the Sistine was Giovanni de Sanctos, who died in 1652. Amann has

said that a *castrato* "could still be heard in St. Peter's in 1896"; see *Allegris Miserere*, p. 35, n. 33. To Fornari, the *castrato* voice was "more pleasant and sweet" than the falsetto, and even "more natural and sincere." Fornari was not fond of the falsetto voice, which he described as "false" because it was "formed in the head"; see Hucke, "Die Besetzung," p. 388, n. 38 and p. 382, n. 9.

47. Schütz, *Historia der frölichen und Siegreichen Aufferstehung unsers einigen Erlösers* (Dresden, 1623; mod. ed. Kassel, 1956), p. [ii].

48. Severi used numbers only in *Beatus vir* (343, $\frac{5}{3}\frac{6}{4}$ and $\frac{5}{4}\frac{}{3}$) and in *Laudate Dominum* (56 and 43).

49. Schütz, *Historia*, p. [ii].

50. The liturgical use and location within the *Liber Usualis* for each piece is given in the Critical Notes.

51. Quoted in Rudolf Walter, "Beziehungen zwischen süddeutscher und italienischer Orgelkunst von tridentinischen Konzil bis zum Ausgang des Barock," *Acta Organologica* V (1971): 164.

52. For *alternatim* use of falsobordoni, see Bradshaw, *The Falsobordone*, pp. 24, 66, 76, and 114.

53. *Caeremoniale episcoporum* (1600); see Walter, "Beziehungen," passim. Earlier, in 1570, it was directed that the text be spoken not in a loud voice (as the *Caeremoniale* of 1600 was to enjoin), but in a soft voice; see Willi Apel, "Probleme der Alternierung in der liturgischen Orgelmusik bis 1600," *Claudio Monteverdi e il suo Tempo* (Verona, 1969), p. 182. In a songbook of 1601 by Bartholomeus Gesius the comment is also made that "it is beautiful and useful if a boy sings along on an organ verset"; see Apel, "Probleme," p. 183.

54. Apel has pointed out that with the numerous organ versets in Banchieri's *L'Organo suonarino* of 1605, the melodies of "the Gregorian chants are often freely changed and even set in completely new ways"; "Probleme," pp. 183-184.

55. Apel, "Probleme," p. 185.

56. See Bradshaw, *The Origin of the Toccata*, pp. 24 and 38. The style of instrumental falsobordoni is discussed in Bradshaw, *The Falsobordone*, pp. 74-78, and a list of pieces is also given. To this list Kastner's publication of eight keyboard falsobordoni, possibly by António Carreira (ca. 1525-ca. 1590), should be added; see *Antonio de Cabezón und Zeitgenossen Kompositionen für Tasteninstrumente* (Frankfurt am Main, 1973), pp. 28-34. I thank Dr. Edward J. Soehnlen for this reference.

57. L. F. Tagliavini, "The Old Italian Organ and Its Music," *The Diapason* 57/3 (February 1966): 14. Many authors speak of this gentle sound. Jeppesen, for instance, in his *Die italienische Orgelmusik am Anfang des Cinquecento* (new rev. ed., Oslo, 1960), I: 16-46, continually used the word "dolcezza" to describe these organs.

58. Costanzo Antegnati, *L'Arte organica* (Brescia, 1608), fol. 7v.

59. In the *Catalogue de la Bibliothèque de F. J. Fétis* (Bruxelles, 1877; repr. ed. Bologna, 1969), the author wrote that Severi's book "contains psalms 'en faux bourdon' with numerous ornaments, rapid scales, groups of different sorts, trills, etc., in one of the voices." He gratuitously added that "this ridiculous practice was introduced into some Roman churches at the beginning of the seventeenth century in imitation of the excessive ornaments used by organists at that time."

60. I thank Dr. R. Münster of the Munich library and Jutta Theurich, research librarian of the Berlin library, for this information.

61. See pp. xii-xiii for advice concerning this practice.

Selected Bibliography

Adami da Bolsena. *Osservazioni per ben regolare il coro dei cantori della cappella pontificia*. Rome: Antonio de'Rossi, 1711.

Amann, Julius. *Allegris Miserere und die Aufführungspraxis in der Sixtina*. Regensburg: Friedrich Pustet, 1935.

Baini, Giuseppe. *Memorie Storico-Critiche della Vita e delle Opere di Giovanni Pierluigi da Palestrina*. Rome: Della Societa Tipografica, 1828. Reprint. Hildesheim: Georg Olms, 1966.

Beyschlag, Adolf. *Die Ornamentik der Musik*. Leipzig: Breitkopf & Härtel, 1908. 2d ed. Leipzig: Breitkopf & Härtel, 1953.

Bradshaw, Murray C. *The Falsobordone, A Study in Renaissance and Baroque Music*. Neuhausen-Stuttgart: Hänssler Verlag, 1978.

Bradshaw, Murray C. *The Origin of the Toccata*. Rome: American Institute of Musicology, 1972.

Brown, Howard M. *Embellishing 16th-Century Music*. London: Oxford University Press, 1976.

Celani, Enrico. "I cantori della Cappella Pontificia nei secoli XVI-XVIII." *Rivista Musicale Italiana* XIV (1907): 752-790.

Chilesotti, Oscar. "Canzonette del Seicento con la Chitarra." *Rivista Musicale Italiana* XVI (1909): 847-862.

Fellerer, Karl Gustav. *The Monody*. Anthology of Music, vol. 31. Cologne: Arno Volk Verlag, 1968.

Ferand, Ernst. "Didactic Embellishment Literature in the Late Renaissance: A Survey of Sources." In *Aspects of Medieval and Renaissance Music*, pp. 154-172. New York, 1966.

Ferand, Ernst. *Die Improvisation in der Musik*. Zurich: Rhein-Verlag, 1938.

Ferand, Ernst. *Improvisation in Nine Centuries of Western Music*. Anthology of Music, vol. 12. Cologne: Arno Volk Verlag, 1961.

Frey, Herman-Walther. "Die Gesänge der Sixtinischen Kapelle an den Sonntagen und Hohen Kirchenfesten des Jahres 1616" *Mélanges Eugène Tisserant* VI (Vatican City, 1964): 395-437.

Gerber, Ernst Ludwig. *Neues historisch-biographisches Lexicon der Tonkünstler*. Leipzig: 1812-1814.

Giazotto, Remo. *Quattro secoli di storia dell'Accademia Nazionale di Santa Cecilia*, vol. 1. Rome: Accademia Nazionale di S. Cecilia, 1970.

Goldschmidt, Hugo. *Die italienische Gesangsmethode des XVII. Jahrhunderts und ihre Bedeutung für die Gegenwart*. Breslau: Schottländer, 1890.

Goldschmidt, Hugo. *Die Lehre von der vokalen Ornamentik*. Charlottenburg: P. Lehsten, 1907.

Haas, Robert. *Aufführungspraxis der Musik*. Potsdam: Athenaion, 1931.

Haas, Robert. *Die Musik des Barocks*. Potsdam: Athenaion, 1928.

Haberl, Franz Xaver. *Bibliographischer und thematischer Musikkatalog der päpstlichen Kapellarchives im Vatikan zu Rom*. Leipzig: 1888.

Haberl, Franz Xaver. "Das traditionelle Musikprogramm der sixtinischen Kapelle nach den Aufzeichnungen von Andrea Adami da Bolsena." *Kirchenmusikalisches Jahrbuch* XII (1897): 36-58.

Hawkins, John. *A General History of the Science and Practice of Music*. London, 1776. Reprint of 1853 ed. New York: Dover, 1963.

Henderson, W. J. *Early History of Singing*. Reprint of 1921 ed. New York: AMS Press, 1969.

Kuhn, Max. *Die Verzierungs-Kunst in der Gesangs-Musik des 16. - 17. Jahrhunderts (1535-1650)*. Leipzig: Breitkopf & Härtel, 1902.

Llorens, Josephus M. *Capellae Sixtinae Codices*. Vatican City: Biblioteca Apostolica Vaticana, 1960.

Pitoni, Giuseppe Ottavio. *Notizia de' Contrapuntisti, e Compositori di Musica*. Early seventeenth century.

Racek, Jan. *Stilprobleme der italienischen Monodie*. Prague: Státní Pedagogické Nakladatelství, 1965.

Schering, Arnold. *Aufführungspraxis alter Musik*. Leipzig: Quelle & Meyer, 1931.

Sievers, G. L. P. "Die päpstliche Kapelle zu Rom." *Allgemeine Musikalische Zeitung* XXIV (1825): 369-378.

Testi, Flavio. *La musica italiana nel medioeva e nel rinascimento*. Milan: Bramante Editrice, 1969.

Timms, Colin. "A Transcription and Detailed Study of Francesco Severi's *Salmi Passaggiati*." Ph.D. dissertation, University of London, 1967.

Ursprung, Otto. *Die katholische Kirchenmusik*. Potsdam: Athenaion, 1931.

Vogel, Emil, and Einstein, Alfred, Lesure, François, and Sartori, Claudio. *Bibliografia della musica italiana vocale profana pubblicata dal 1500 al 1700*. New edition. Pomezia: Staderini-Minkoff, 1977.

Walther, Johann G. *Musikalisches Lexicon*. Leipzig, 1732. Facsimile edition. Kassel: Bärenreiter, 1953.

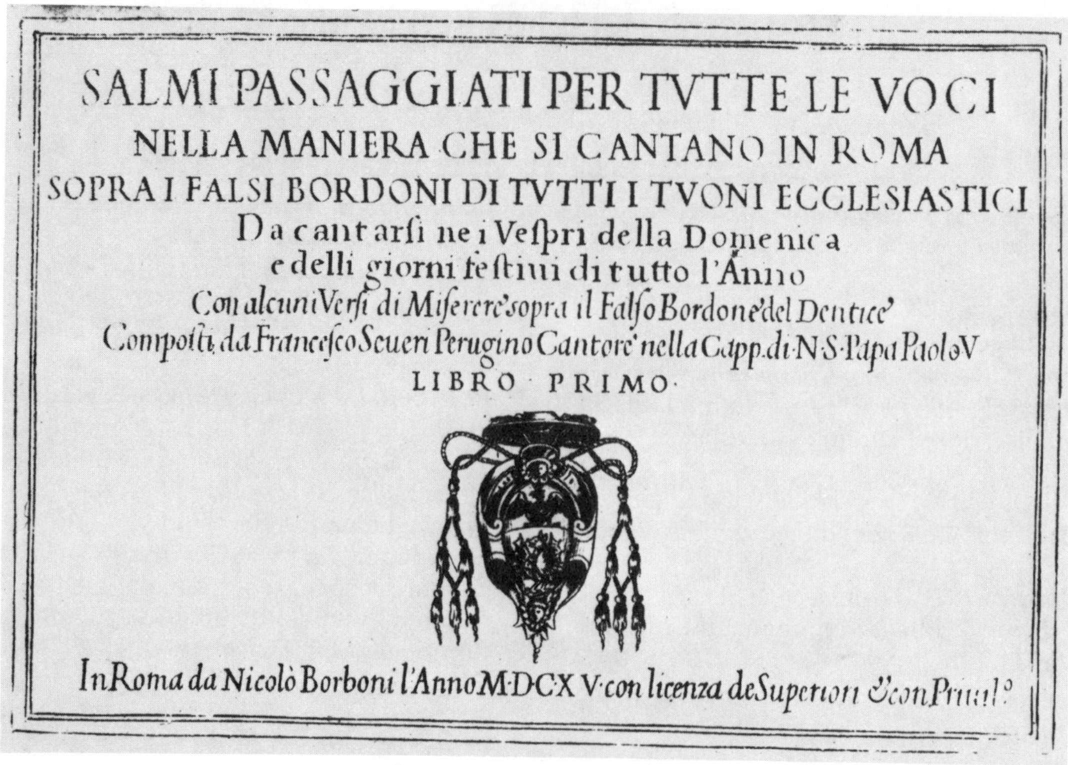

SALMI PASSAGGIATI PER TVTTE LE VOCI
NELLA MANIERA CHE SI CANTANO IN ROMA
SOPRA I FALSI BORDONI DI TVTTI I TVONI ECCLESIASTICI
Da cantarsi ne i Vespri della Domenica
e delli giorni festiui di tutto l'Anno
Con alcuni Versi di Miserere sopra il Falso Bordone del Dentice
Composti da Francesco Seueri Perugino Cantore nella Capp. di N.S. Papa Paolo V
LIBRO PRIMO
In Roma da Nicolò Borboni l'Anno M.DCXV con licenza de Superiori & con Priuil.°

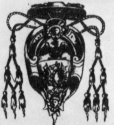

Plate I. Francesco Severi, *Salmi passaggiati* (1615), title page.
(Courtesy, The British Library)

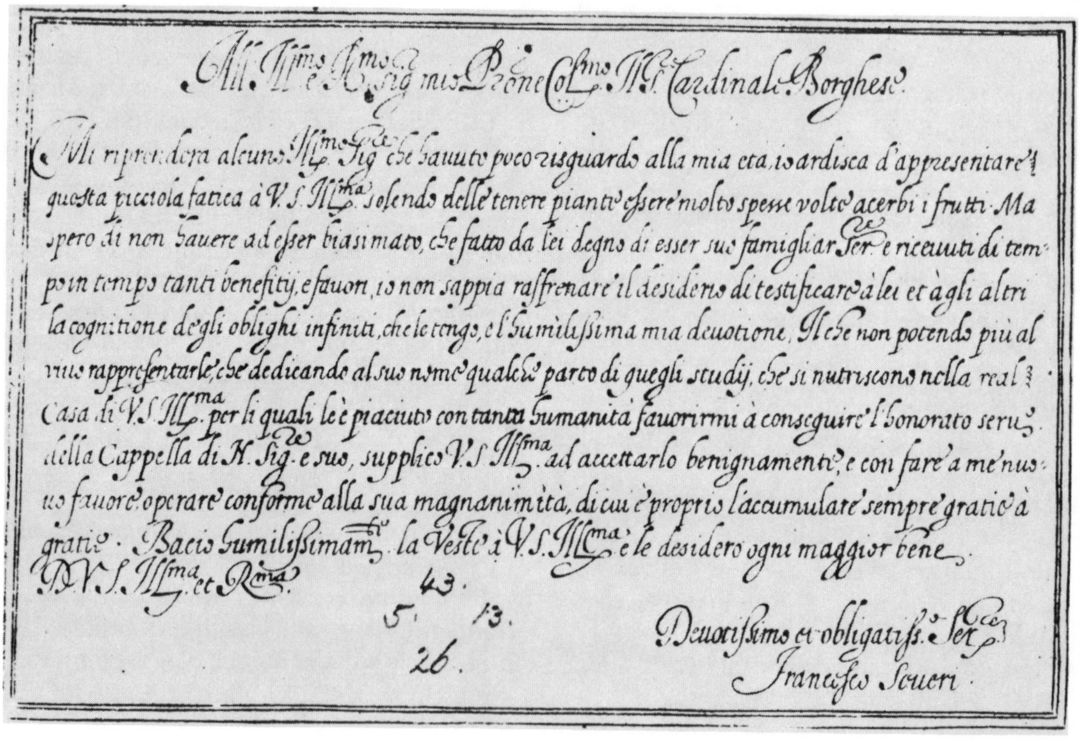

All'Ill.mo e R.mo Sig.r mio P.rone Col.mo Il S.r Cardinale Borghese.

Mi riprenderà alcuno Ill.mo Sig.r che hauuto poco risguardo alla mia età, io ardisca d'appresentare questa picciola fatica à V.S. Ill.ma solendo delle tenere piante essere molto spesse volte acerbi i frutti. Ma spero di non hauere ad esser biasimato, che fatto da lei degno di esser suo famigliar Ser.re e riceuuti di tempo in tempo tanti benefitij, e fauori, io non sappia raffrenare il desiderio di testificare à lei et à gli altri la cognitione degli oblighi infiniti, che le tengo, e l'humilissima mia deuotione. Il che non potendo più al viuo rappresentarle, che dedicando al suo nome qualche parto di quegli studij, che si nutriscono nella real Casa di V.S. Ill.ma per li quali le è piaciuto con tanta humanità fauorirmi à conseguire l'honorato seruitio della Cappella di N. Sig.re suo, supplico V.S. Ill.ma ad accettarlo benignamente, e con fare a me nuouo fauore operare conforme alla sua magnanimità, di cui è proprio l'accumulare sempre gratie à gratie. Bacio humilissimam.te la Veste à V.S. Ill.ma e le desidero ogni maggior bene.

Di V.S. Ill.ma et R.ma

Deuotissimo et obligatiss.o Ser.re
Francesco Seueri

Plate II. Francesco Severi, *Salmi passaggiati* (1615), dedication.
(Courtesy, The British Library)

EMBELLISHED PSALMS FOR ALL VOICES

ACCORDING TO THE WAY THEY ARE SUNG IN ROME
ON THE FALSOBORDONE OF ALL THE ECCLESIASTICAL TONES

To be sung at Sunday Vespers
and feast days throughout the year
together with some verses of the Miserere, on a Falsobordone by Dentice,
Composed by Francesco Severi of Perugia, Singer in the Chapel of our Holiness, Pope Paul V

Book One

[Borghese coat of arms with Cardinal's hat]

In Rome, by Nicolò Borboni, 1615, with Superiors' permission and with privilege

[Dedication]

To my patron, the most illustrious Cardinal Scipione Borghese,

I recall, most illustrious Lord, that you had little concern about my youthfulness, and so I venture to present to your most illustrious Lordship this small effort, even though habitually the fruit of tender plants is harsh. I hope I am not censured in this since I have been considered worthy to be your familiar servant and have often received many benefits and favors. I do not know how to curb the desire I have to declare both to you and to others my recognition of the great obligation I owe you, as well as my most humble devotion. I know not how to do this save by dedicating to your name this book, which is the fruit of those studies nourished in the princely house of your Excellency, during which time you were pleased with great kindness to assist me, your obedient servant, in entering the chapel of His Holiness. I beseech your most Illustrious Lordship kindly to accept it and so do me a new kindness which but accords with your magnanimity, which continues to gather more and more good will. Most humbly do I kiss your garment, and desire for you every good.

Your most obedient and devoted servant,
Francesco Severi

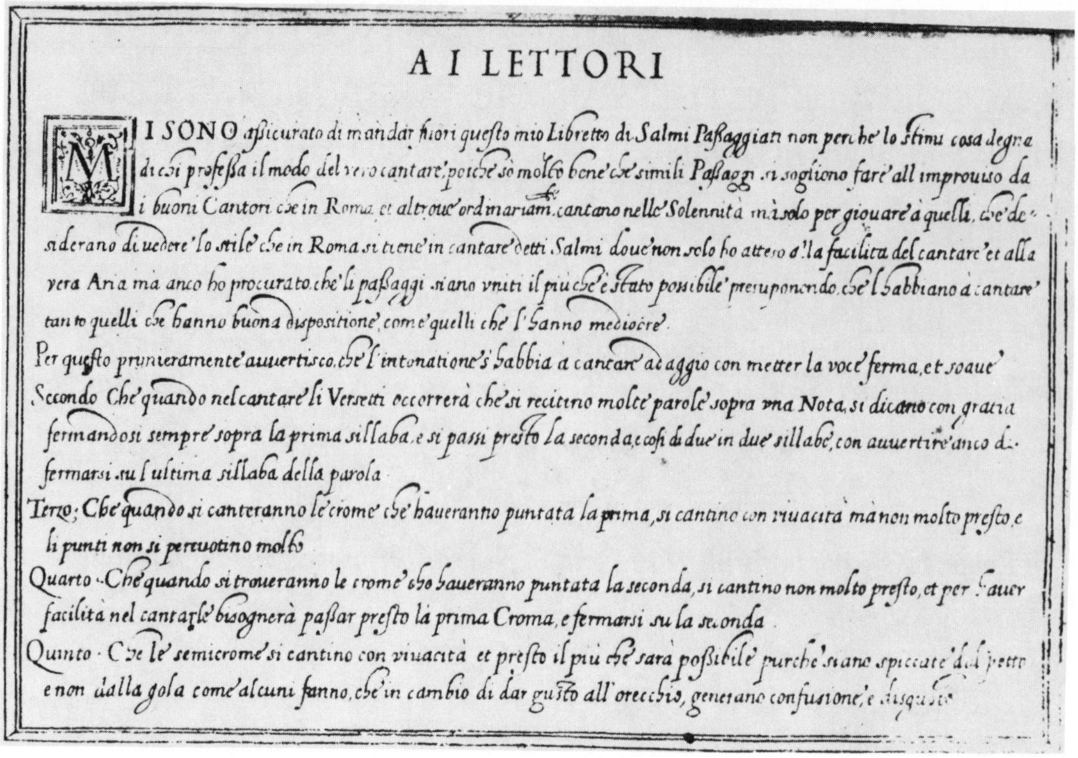

A I LETTORI

MI SONO assicurato di mandar fuori questo mio Libretto di Salmi Passaggiati non perche lo stimi cosa degna di cosi professa il modo del vero cantare, poiche so molto bene che simili Passaggi si sogliono fare all'improuiso da i buoni Cantori che in Roma et altroue ordinariam. cantano nelle Solennità ma solo per giouare à quelli, che desiderano di uedere lo stile che in Roma si tiene in cantare detti Salmi doue non solo ho atteso alla facilità del cantare et alla vera Aria ma anco ho procurato che li passaggi siano vniti il piu che è stato possibile presuponendo che l'habbiano à cantare tanto quelli che hanno buona dispositione, come quelli che l'hanno mediocre.

Per questo primieramente auuertisco che l'intonatione s'habbia à cantare adagio con metter la voce ferma, et soaue.

Secondo Che quando nel cantare li Versetti occorrerà che si recitino molte parole sopra vna Nota, si dicano con gratia fermandosi sempre sopra la prima sillaba, e si passi presto la seconda, e cosi di due in due sillabe, con auuertire anco di fermarsi su l'ultima sillaba della parola.

Terzo; Che quando si canteranno le crome che haueranno puntata la prima, si cantino con viuacità ma non molto presto, e li punti non si percuotino molto.

Quarto Che quando si trouerannno le crome che haueranno puntata la seconda, si cantino non molto presto, et per hauer facilità nel cantarle bisognerà passar presto la prima Croma, e fermarsi su la seconda.

Quinto Che le semicrome si cantino con viuacità et presto il più che sarà possibile purche siano spiccate dal petto e non dalla gola come alcuni fanno, che in cambio di dar gusto all'orecchio, generano confusione, e disgusto.

Plate III. Francesco Severi, *Salmi passaggiati* (1615), To the Readers.
(Courtesy, The British Library)

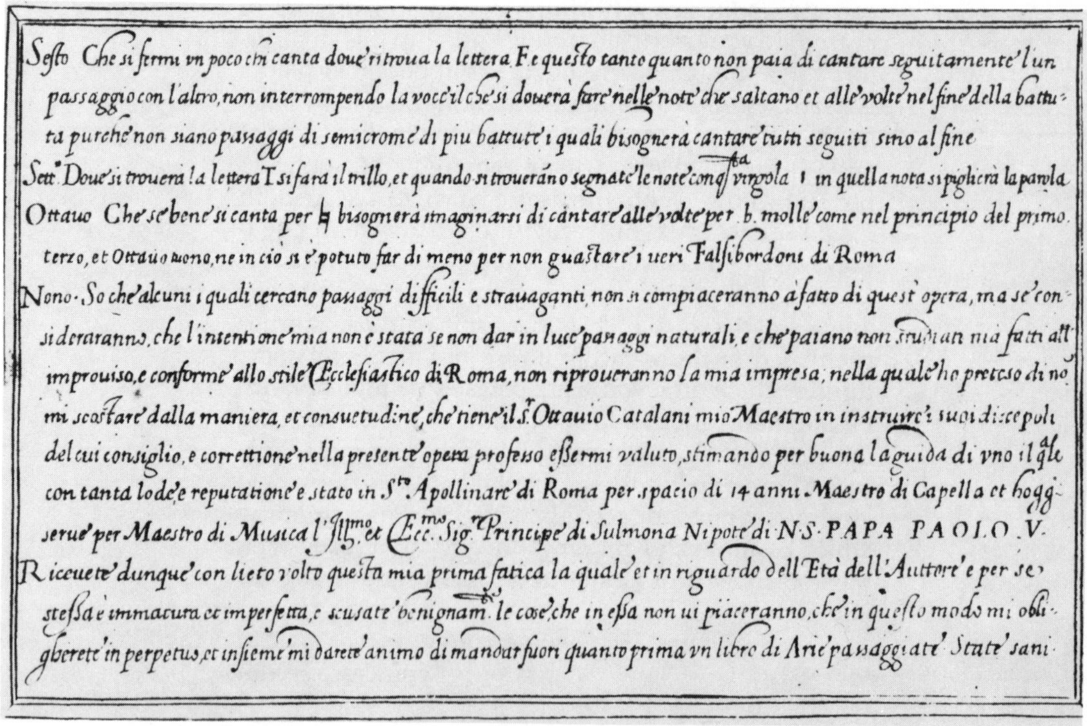

Sesto Che si fermi vn poco chi canta doue ritroua la lettera F e questo tanto quanto non paia di cantare seguitamente l'un passaggio con l'altro, non interrompendo la voce il che si douerà fare nelle note che saltano et alle volte nel fine della battuta purche non siano passaggi di semicrome di piu battute i quali bisognerà cantare tutti seguiti sino al fine.

Sett. Doue si trouerà la lettera T si farà il trillo, et quando si trouerano segnate le note con questa virgola ı in quella nota si piglierà la parola.

Ottauo Che se bene si canta per ♮ bisognerà imaginarsi di cantare alle volte per b. molle come nel principio del primo. terzo, et Ottauo tuono, ne in ciò si è potuto far di meno per non guastare i ueri Falsibordoni di Roma.

Nono. So che alcuni i quali cercano passaggi difficili e strauaganti, non si compiaceranno affatto di quest'opera, ma se consideraranno, che l'intentione mia non è stata se non dar in luce passaggi naturali, e che paiano non studiati ma fatti all'improuiso, e conforme allo stile Ecclesiastico di Roma, non riprouerranno la mia impresa, nella quale ho preteso di non mi scostare dalla maniera, et consuetudine, che tiene il S. Ottauio Catalani mio Maestro in instruire i suoi discepoli del cui consiglio, e correttione nella presente opera professo essermi valuto, stimando per buona la guida di vno il qle con tanta lode e reputatione è stato in S. Apollinare di Roma per spatio di 14 anni Maestro di Capella et hoggi serue per Maestro di Musica l'Illmo. et Eccmo. Sig. Principe di Sulmona Nipote di N.S. PAPA PAOLO V.

Riceuete dunque con lieto volto questa mia prima fatica la quale et in riguardo dell'Età dell'Auttore e per se stessa è immatura et imperfetta, e scusate benignam. le cose, che in essa non ui piaceranno, che in questo modo mi obligherete in perpetuo, et insieme mi darete animo di mandar fuori quanto prima vn libro di Arie passaggiate. State sani.

Plate IV. Francesco Severi, *Salmi passaggiati* (1615), To the Readers.
(Courtesy, The British Library)

To the readers,

I am confident in sending forth this little book of embellished psalms not because I esteem it worthy of those who practice the manner of correct singing, since I well know that similar *passaggi* are customarily improvised by good singers in Rome and elsewhere when they sing services, but because I wish only to please those who desire to see the style adhered to in Rome in singing psalms. Thus I not only have been concerned about facility in singing and the true type of song, but have used embellishments that are as far as possible uniform, assuming that they are to be sung by those who have a good as well as a mediocre talent.

I suggest first of all that the intonation [the first verse of every piece] be sung *adagio*, with a firm and sweet voice.

Second, if when singing the verses it should happen that there are many words on a single note [during recitations], they should be sung gracefully, always holding the first syllable and passing quickly over the second one, and so on with every two syllables. Take care to hold the last syllable of a word.

Third, when *crome* are sung that have a dot on the first one, they are sung in a lively way, but not too quickly, and the dots are not emphasized too much.

Fourth, when there are *crome* that have a dot on the second one, they are not sung too quickly. To gain ease in singing, it will be necessary to pass quickly over the first *croma* and hold the second one.

Fifth, *semicrome* are sung in a lively and quick way. This can be done only if they are sung from the chest and not from the throat, as some do who in trying to please our ears only confuse and disgust us.

Sixth, the singer should stop when he comes across the letter F; this is because some performers sing one *passaggio* right after another, not breaking the voice, which they should do on notes that leap and some-times at the end of a beat, provided that the *passaggi* do not consist of *semicrome* that go beyond the beat. In this case the performer should be careful to sing everything up to the end.

Seventh, when the letter T is used, one should sing a *trillo*; and when notes have a *virgola*, ⎮ , one should sing a syllable on that note.

Eighth, although a B-natural is often written, one should sometime imagine a B-flat, as in the beginning of the first, third, and eighth tones. By observing this, one at least will not destroy the true falsobordoni of Rome.

Ninth, I know there are some who attempt difficult and inordinate embellishments that do not comply with this work, but if you consider that my intention has been not only to publish embellishments that seem natural and improvised, but which also conform to the ecclesiastical style of Rome, you should not find fault with my undertaking.

In it I have not attempted to put aside the method and practice which Ottavio Catalano, my master, follows in teaching his students. I confess that his advice and criticism in the present volume have been of great value to me. I esteem highly the guidance of one who for fourteen years served at San Apollinare in Rome with so much honor and fame, and who today serves as music master for the most illustrious and excellent Prince of Sulmona, the nephew of our Holiness, Pope Paul V.

Receive, then, with kind regard this first effort of mine, which both in itself and because of the age of the author is immature and imperfect. Pardon, kind reader, the things that do not please you in it. In this way you place me forever in your debt and encourage me to send forth even sooner a book of embellished songs.

May you have good health.

Plate V. Francesco Severi, *Salmi passaggiati* (1615), p. 66.
(Courtesy, The British Library)

SALMI PASSAGGIATI (1615)

[1] Dixit Dominus
Primo tuono

Intonatione del primo tuono

Dixit   1. Di-   xit_____ Dó- mi- nus Dó-   mi- no   me-

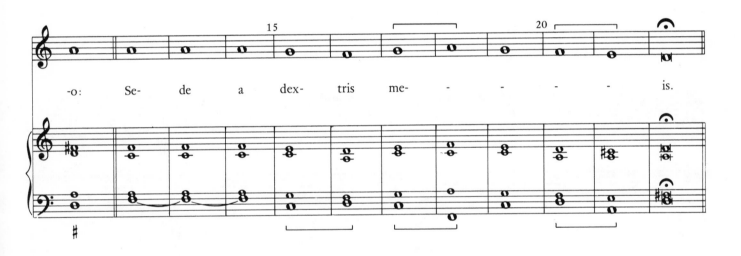

-o: Se-   de   a   dex- tris   me-   — — — —   is.

Falsobordone del primo tuono

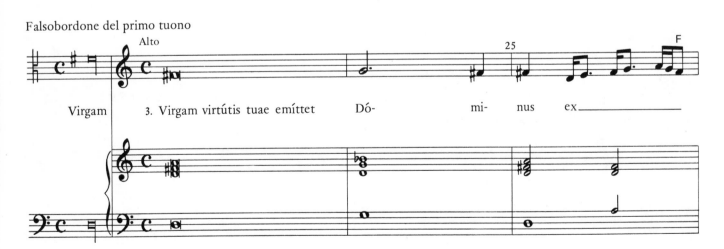

Virgam   3. Virgam virtútis tuae emíttet   Dó-   mi-   nus   ex_____

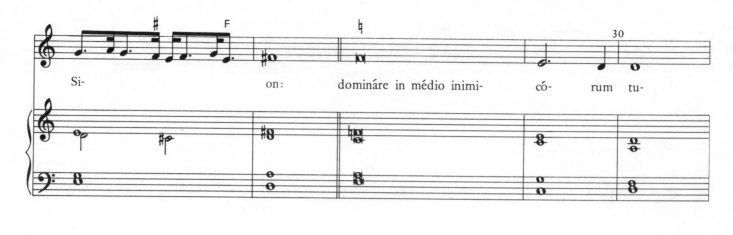

Si-
on:
domináre in médio inimi-
có-
rum tu-

-ó-

rum.

Juravit
5. Jurávit Dóminus, et non pae-
ni-
té-

bit e-   um:

Tu es sacérdos in aetérnum secúndum órdi-   nem Mel-

chí-   se-   dech.

Judicabit 7. Judicábit in natióni- bus, im- plé- bit ru-

-í- nas: conquassábit cápi- ta in_____ ter- ra mul-

-tó- - - -

- - - rum.

Gloria

9. Glo- ri- a Pa-

-tri, et_____ Fí- li- o,

et_____ Spi- rí- tu- i

San-

85

cto.

[Canto]

F

Sicut   10. Sicut erat in princípi-   o,   et_____ nunc,_____

_____ et_____ sem-   per,

et_____ in saécula saecu-   ló-

Chant verses for *alternatim* performance.

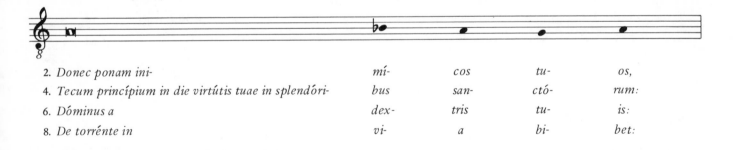

2. *Donec ponam ini-*   mí-   cos   tu-   os,
4. *Tecum princípium in die virtútis tuae in splendóri-* bus   san-   ctó-   rum:
6. *Dóminus a*   dex-   tris   tu-   is:
8. *De torrénte in*   vi-   a   bi-   bet:

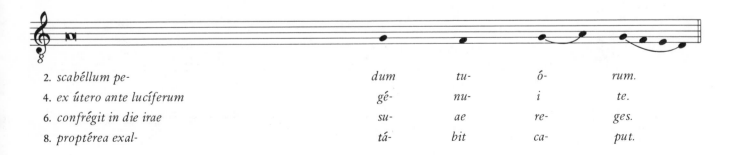

2. *scabéllum pe-*   dum   tu-   ó-   rum.
4. *ex útero ante lucíferum*   gé-   nu-   i   te.
6. *confrégit in die irae*   su-   ae   re-   ges.
8. *proptérea exal-*   tá-   bit   ca-   put.

8

[2] Confitebor tibi Domine
Secondo tuono

Intonatione del secondo tuono

Confitebor 1. Con- - fi- tébor tibi Dómine in toto cor- de

me- o: in consílio justórum et congre- ga- ti- ó- ne.

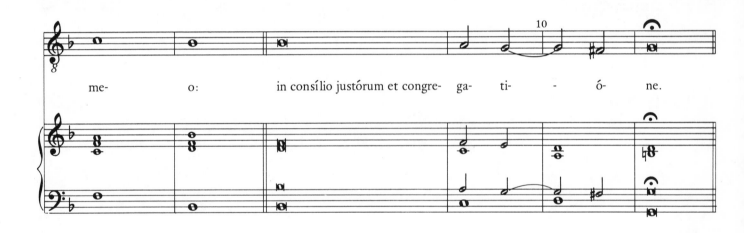

Falsobordone del secondo tuono

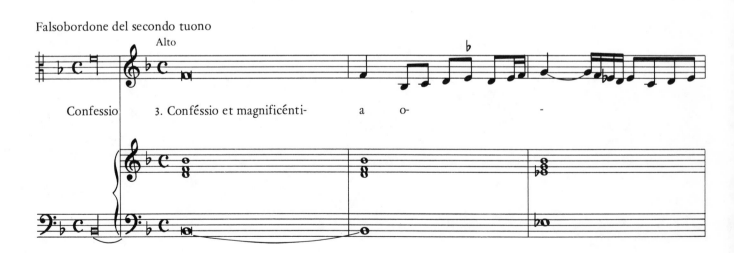

Confessio 3. Conféssio et magnificénti- a o-

- pus_____ e- jus: et justítia ejus manet in saé- cu-lum

saé- - cu- li.

Memor 5. Memor erit in saécu- lum te- - sta-

-mén- - -

- ti_____ su- i: virtútem óperum suórum annuntiábit pó-

- - pu-lo su- o:

Fidelia 7. Fidélia ómnia mandáta ejus: confirmáta in saé-

- cu-lum saé- - cu- li: facta in veritáte et

ae- qui- tá- - te.

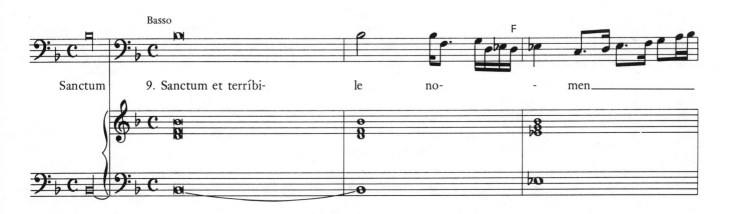

Basso

Sanctum   9. Sanctum et terríbi- le no- - men_____

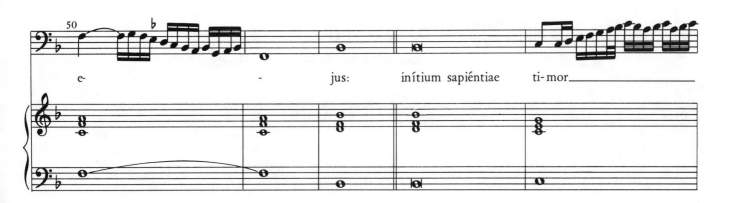

e- - jus: inítium sapiéntiae ti-mor_____

Dó- - - mi- ni.

Gloria 11. Glóri- a Pa- tri, et _____

_____ Fí- li- o, et Spíritu- i San-

- - - cto.

Sicut 12. Sicut erat in princípi- o, et_____ nunc, et_____

sem- per,

et in saécula saeculó- rum. A-

men.

Chant verses for *alternatim* performance.

			Dó-	mi-	ni:
2. *Magna ópera*					
4. *Memóriam fecit mirabílium*	*suó- rum,*	*miséricors et miserátor*	*Dó-*	*mi-*	*nus:*
6. *Ut det illis haereditátem*			*gén-*	*ti-*	*um:*
8. *Redemptiónem misit pópulo*			*su-*		*o:*
10. *Intelléctus bonus ómnibus faciéntibus*			*e-*		*um:*

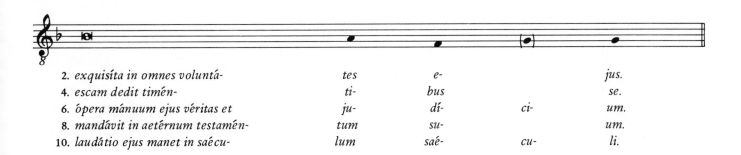

2. *exquisíta in omnes voluntá-*	*tes*	*e-*		*jus.*
4. *escam dedit timén-*	*ti-*	*bus*		*se.*
6. *ópera mánuum ejus véritas et*	*ju-*	*dí-*	*ci-*	*um.*
8. *mandávit in aetérnum testamén-*	*tum*	*su-*		*um.*
10. *laudátio ejus manet in saécu-*	*lum*	*saé-*	*cu-*	*li.*

[3] Beatus vir
Terzo tuono

Intonatione del 3° tuono

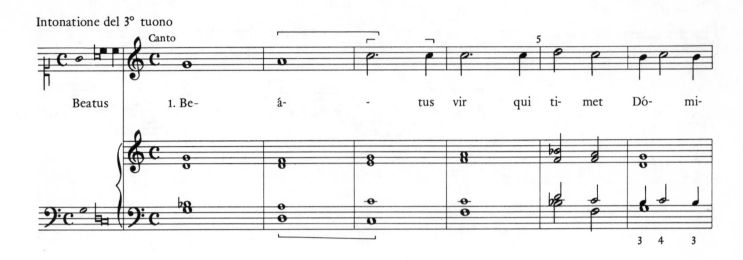

Beatus   1. Be- á- tus vir qui ti- met Dó- mi-

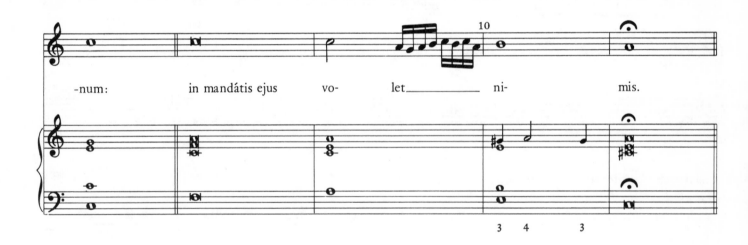

-num: in mandátis ejus vo- let_____ ni- mis.

Falsobordone del 3° tuono

Gloria   3. Glória et divítiae in   do-

-mo e- - - jus:

et justítia ejus manet in saéculum saé-

- - cu- li.

Jocundus 5. Jucúndus homo qui miserétur et cómmodat, dispónet sermónes suos in ju-

-dí- ci- o: quia in aetérnum non com- mo-

-vé- - bi- tur.

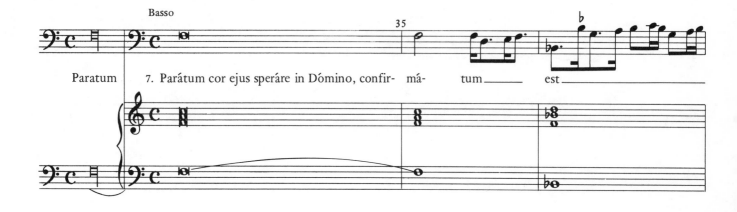

Paratum 7. Parátum cor ejus speráre in Dómino, confir- má- tum_____ est_____

_ cor_____ e- - jus:

non commovébitur donec despíciat ini- mí- cos

su- os.

Tenore

Peccator 9. Peccátor vidébit, et irascétur, déntibus suis fremet et

ta- bé- scet: desidérium peccatórum pe-

-rí- - - bit.

Gloria   10. Glória   Pa-   tri,   et _____ Fí-   li-

-o,   et Spi- rí- tu- i San- - cto.

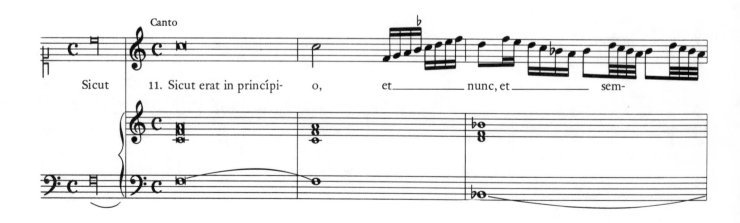

Sicut   11. Sicut erat in princípi-   o,   et _____ nunc, et _____ sem-

-      -   -   -   per,

et in saécula saeculórum. A-   -   men.

Chant verses for *alternatim* performance.

		se-	men	e-	jus:
2. *Potens in terra erit*					
4. *Exórtum est in ténebris*		lu-	men	re-	ctis:
6. *In memória aetérna*		e-	rit	ju-	stus:
8. *Dispérsit, dedit pau- pé- ri- bus:*	*justitia ejus manet in saé-*	*cu-*	*lum*	*saé-*	*cu-*	*li:*

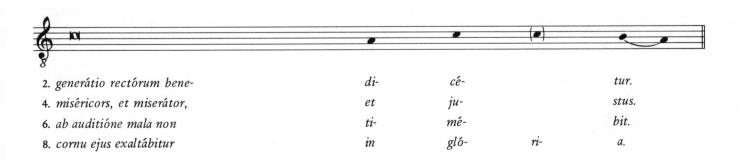

	di-	cé-	tur.
2. *generátio rectórum bene-*			
4. *miséricors, et miserátor,*	et	ju-	stus.
6. *ab auditióne mala non*	ti-	mé-	bit.
8. *cornu ejus exaltábitur*	in	gló- ri-	a.

[4] Laudate pueri
Quarto tuono

Intonatione del 4° tuono

Laudate 1. Lau- dá- te pú- e- ri Dó-

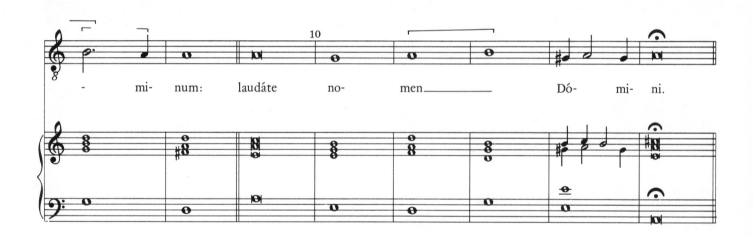

-mi- num: laudáte no- men_____ Dó- mi- ni.

Falsobordone del 4° tuono

A 3. A solis ortu usque ad___ oc- cá-

sum, laudábile no- men____ Dó- - - mi- ni.

Canto

Quis 5. Quis sicut Dóminus Deus noster, qui in____ al- tis

há- - bi- tat,

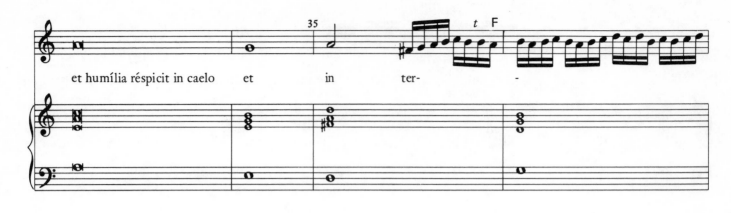

et humília réspicit in caelo et in ter-

- - -ra?

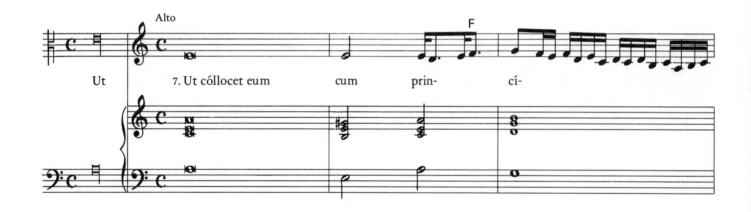

Ut 7. Ut cóllocet eum cum prin- cí-

-pi- bus, cum princípibus

pó-   pu- li su-

—   —   i.

Canto

Gloria   9. Glória   Pa-   -   tri,

et _____   Fí-   li-   o,   et _____

Spi- rí- tu- i San- -

- cto.

[Canto]

Sicut 10. Sicut erat in princípio, et _____ nunc,

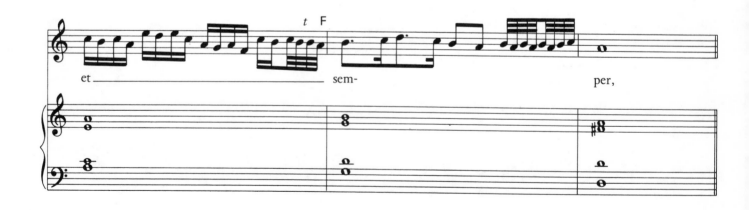

et _____ sem- per,

et in saécula saecu- ló- rum. A-

men.

Chant verses for *alternatim* performance.

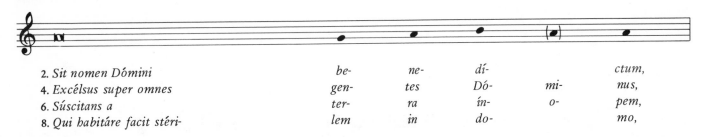

2. *Sit nomen Dómini*		be-	ne-	dí-		ctum,
4. *Excélsus super omnes*		gen-	tes	Dó-	mi-	nus,
6. *Súscitans a*		ter-	ra	ín-	o-	pem,
8. *Qui habitáre facit stéri-*		lem	in	do-		mo,

2. *ex hoc nunc, et*	us-	que	in	saé-	cu-	lum.
4. *et super caelos*	gló-	ri-	a		e-	jus.
6. *et de stércore*	é-	ri-	gens	paú-	pe-	rem.
8. *matrem fili-*	ó-	rum	lae-		tán-	tem.

[5] Laudate Dominum
Quinto tuono

Intonatione del 5° tuono

Laudate   1. Lau- dá- te Dó- - mi- num o- mnes gen-

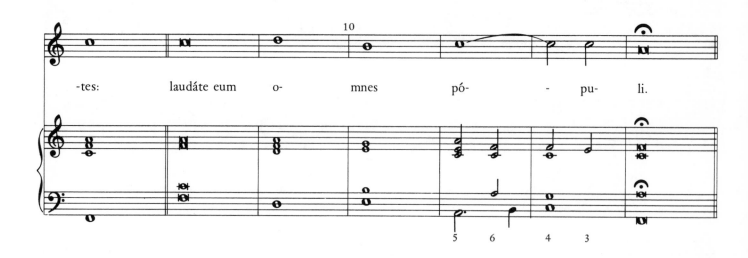

-tes: laudáte eum o- mnes pó- - pu- li.

Falsobordone del 5° tuono

Quoniam   2. Quóniam confirmáta est super nos miseri- cór- di- a_____ e-

jus: et véritas Dómini manet

in   ae-   tér-   -   num.

Gloria   3. Glória Patri,   et_____   Fí-

-           li-   o,   et Spi-   rí-   tu- i_____

San- - cto.

Sicut 4. Sicut erat in princípio, et nunc, et

sem- per, et in saécula saecu- ló- rum. A-

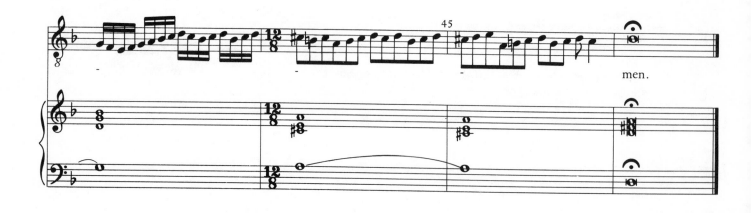

- - - men.

[6] Magnificat
Sesto tuono

Intonatione del 6° tuono

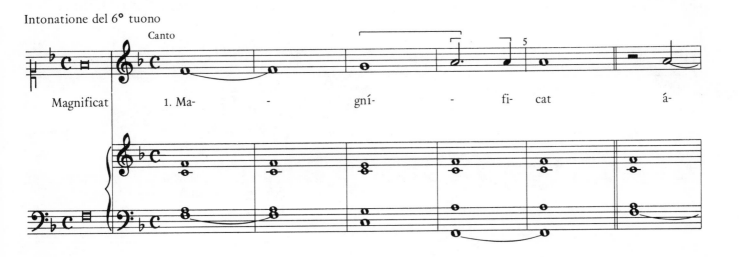

Magnificat   1. Ma-   gní-   fi- cat   á-

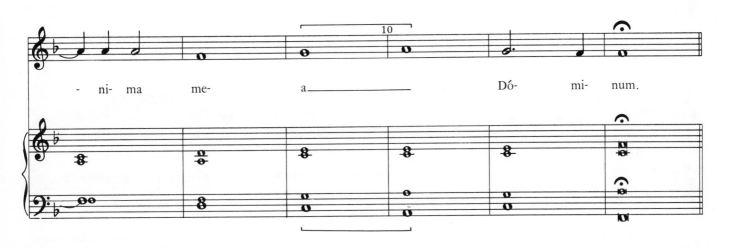

-ni- ma me-   a_____ Dó- mi- num.

Falsobordone del 6° tuono

Tenore

Quia   3. Quia respéxit humilitátem ancíl- lae_____ su-

ae: ecce enim ex hoc beátam me dicent omnes gene-

-ra-   -   -

-                ti-   ó-   -   -

-                         -   F

nes.

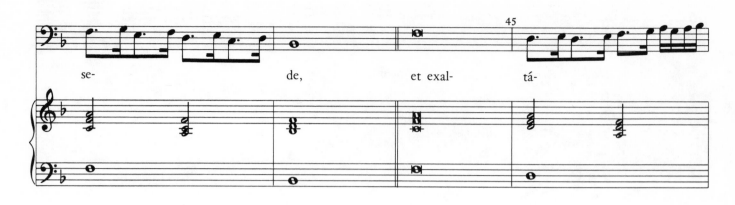

se- de, et exal- tá-

- vit hú- mi- les.

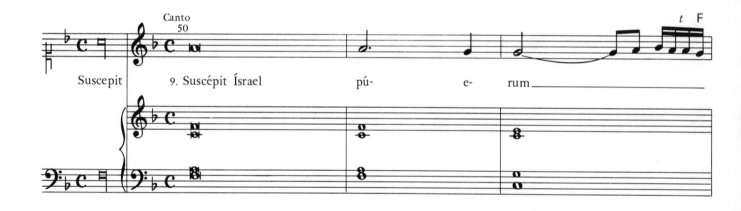

Suscepit 9. Suscépit Ísrael pú- e- rum

su- um, recordátus miseri-

-rí- tu- i San- - - - cto.

Canto

Sicut 12. Sicut erat in princípi- o, et_____ nunc, et_____ sem-

- per, et in saécula sae- cu-

Chant verses for *alternatim* performance.

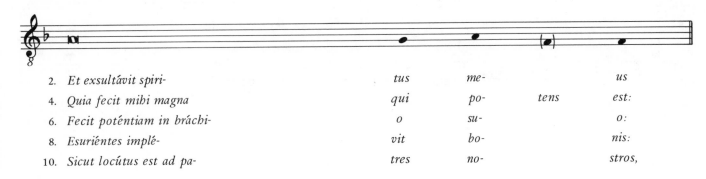

	tus	me-		us
2. *Et exsultávit spiri-*	tus	me-		us
4. *Quia fecit mihi magna*	qui	po-	tens	est:
6. *Fecit poténtiam in bráchi-*	o	su-		o:
8. *Esuriéntes implé-*	vit	bo-		nis:
10. *Sicut locútus est ad pa-*	tres	no-		stros,

2. *in Deo salu-*	tá-	ri	me-	o.
4. *et sanctum*	no-	men	e-	jus.
6. *dispérsit supérbos mente*	cor-	dis	su-	i.
8. *et dívites dimí-*	sit	in-	á-	nes.
10. *Ábraham et sémini e-*	jus	in	saé-cu-	la.

[7] Nisi Dominus
Settimo tuono

Intonatione del 7° tuono

Nisi   1. Ni-   si_____   Dóminus aedifi- cá- ve- rit   do-

-mum,   in va-   num laboravérunt qui ae- dí-   fi- cant   e -   am.

Falsobordone del 7° tuono

Vanum   3. Vanum est vobis   an- te_____ lu-

-cem súr- - ge- re: súrgite postquam sedéritis, qui manducátis

pa- nem do- ló- - ris.

Canto

Sicut 5. Sicut sagíttae in ma- nu pó-

-tén- tis: ita fílii ex-

-cus- só- - - rum.

Basso

Gloria 7. Glóri- a Pa- -

-tri, et Fí- li- o, et Spi-

-rí- tu- i San- - cto.

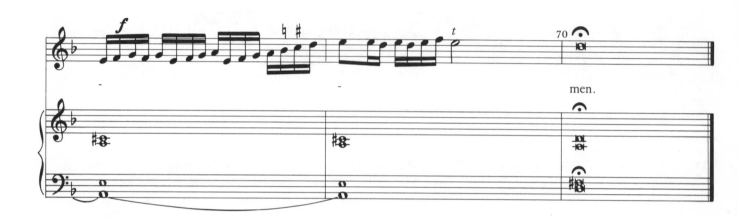

Chant verses for *alternatim* performance.

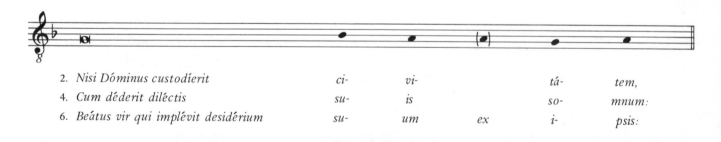

2. *Nisi Dóminus custodíerit*   ci-   vi-   tá-   tem,
4. *Cum déderit diléctis*   su-   is   so-   mnum:
6. *Beátus vir qui implévit desidérium*   su-   um   ex   i-   psis:

2. *frustra vígilat qui cu-*   stó-   dit   e-   am.
4. *ecce haeréditas Dómini, fílii: merces,*   fru-   ctus   ven-   tris.
6. *non confundétur cum loquétur inimícis*   su-   is   in   por-   ta.

[8] In convertendo
Ottavo tuono

Intonatione del 8° tuono

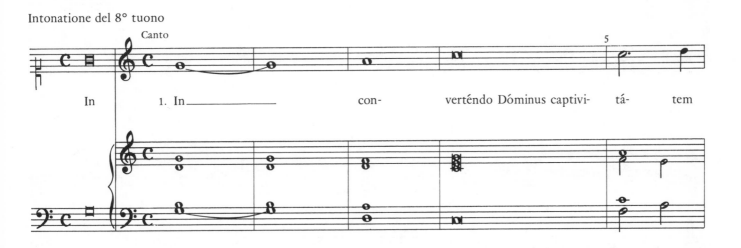

In

1. In_____ con- verténdo Dóminus captivi- tá- tem

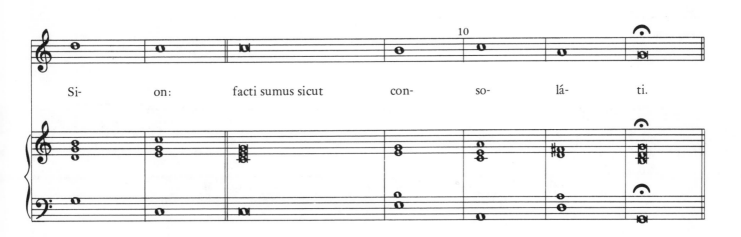

Si- on: facti sumus sicut con- so- lá- ti.

Falsobordone del 8° tuono

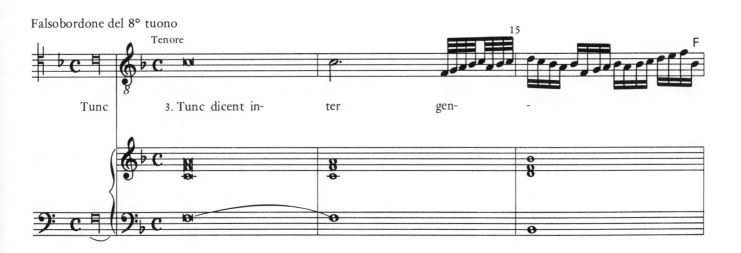

Tunc 3. Tunc dicent in- ter gen-

-tes: Magnificávit Dóminus   fá-   ce-   re   no-
-bís-   cum.

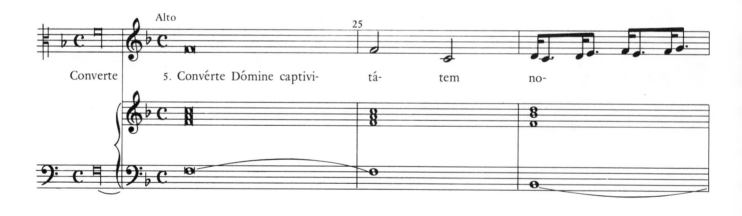

Converte   5. Convérte Dómine captivi-   tá-   tem   no-

- stram,_____

sicut tor- rens in Aú- -stro. _____

Basso

Euntes 7. Eúntes ibant et fle- -

- bant, mitténtes sé- - mi- na _____

et in saécula saecu- ló-   rum. A-

-                    -   -   men.

Chant verses for *alternatim* performance.

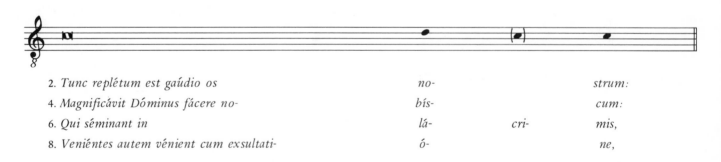

2. *Tunc replétum est gaúdio os*   *no-*   *strum:*
4. *Magnificávit Dóminus fácere no-*   *bís-*   *cum:*
6. *Qui séminant in*   *lá-*   *cri-*   *mis,*
8. *Veniéntes autem vénient cum exsultati-*   *ó-*   *ne,*

2. *et lingua nostra exsul-*   *ta-*   *ti-*   *ó-*   *ne.*
4. *facti su-*   *mus*   *lae-*   *tán-*   *tes.*
6. *in exsultati-*   *ó-*   *ne*   *me-*   *tent.*
8. *portántes maní-*   *pu-*   *los*   *su-*   *os.*

[9] In exitu

Misto tuono

Intonatione del misto tuono

In   1. In_____ éx- i- tu Ís- ra- el de

Ae- gý- pto,   domus Jacob   de pó- - pu-lo bár- ba- ro:_____

Falsobordone del misto tuono

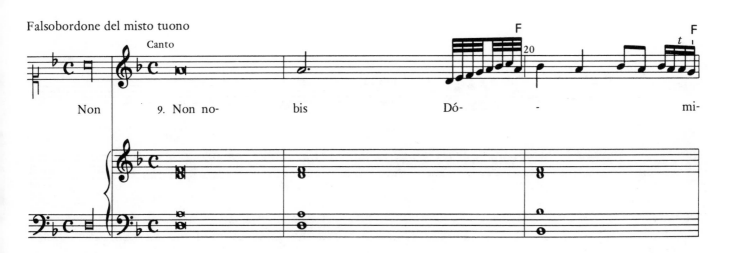

Non   9. Non no-   bis   Dó- - mi-

-ne, non _____ no- bis, sed nómini tu- o da _____

_ gló- - - ri- am.

Basso
Deus 11. Deus autem no- -

- ster in cae- lo: ómnia quaecúmque vóluit,

fe- - - cit.

Os 13. Os habent, et non _____ lo- quén-

- - - tur:

óculos habent, et non vi- dé- -

50

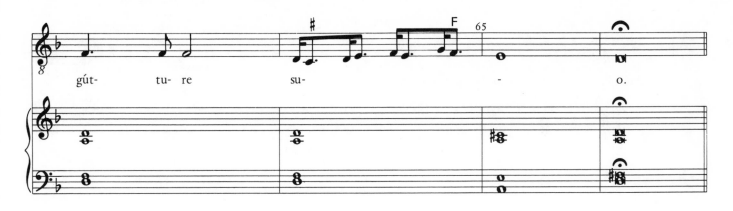

gút- tu- re su- - o.

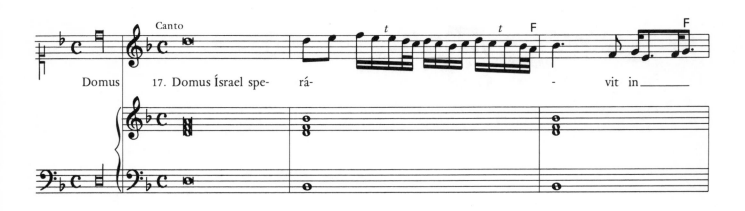

Domus 17. Domus Ísrael spe- rá- - vit in

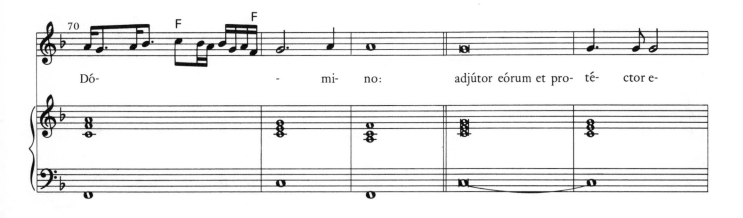

Dó- - mi- no: adjútor eórum et pro- té- ctor e-

-ó- - rum est.

Qui

19. Qui timent Dóminum spera- vé-

- -runt in Dó- mi- no:

adjútor eórum et protéctor e- ó- -

- - rum est.

54

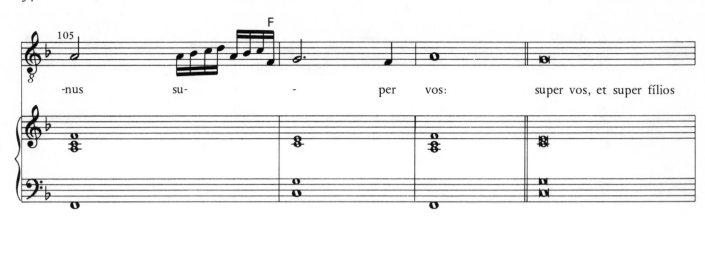

-nus su- - per vos: super vos, et super fílios

ve- - - stros.

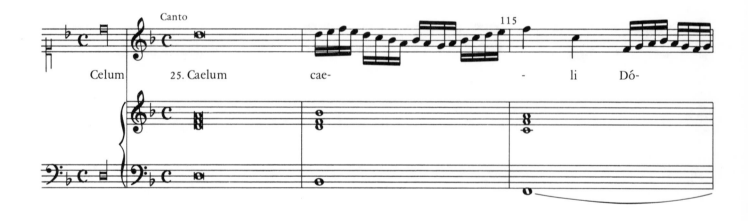

Celum   25. Caelum   cae- - li   Dó-

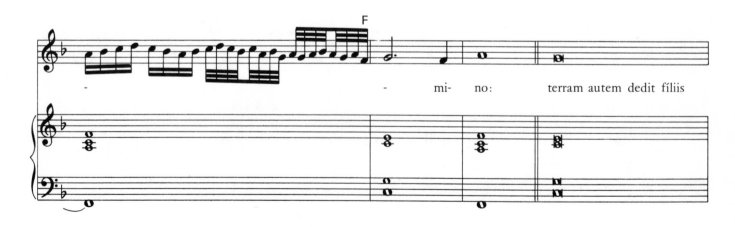

- mi- no: terram autem dedit fíliis

hó- - mi- num.

Alto

Sed 27. Sed nos qui vívimus, benedícimus Dó-

- - mi- no,

ex hoc nunc et usque in saé- -

cu- lum.

à2 Soprani

Sicut   29. Sicut erat in princípio,   et_____ nunc, et sem-

Sicut   29. Sicut erat in princípio,   et_____ nunc,_____ et

-    -   -   per,

sem-   -   -   per,

et in saécula saeculórum. A-

et in saécula saeculórum. A-

men.

men.

Chant verses for *alternatim* performance.

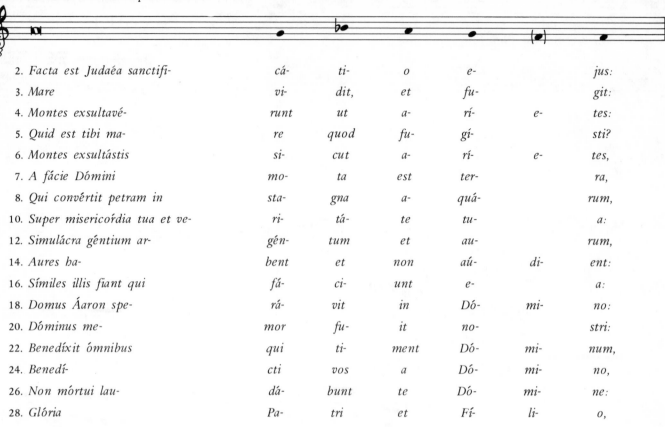

2. *Facta est Judaéa sanctifi-*	cá-	ti-	o	e-	jus:
3. *Mare*	vi-	dit,	et	fu-	git:
4. *Montes exsultavé-*	runt	ut	a-	rí- e-	tes:
5. *Quid est tibi ma-*	re	quod	fu-	gí-	sti?
6. *Montes exsultástis*	si-	cut	a-	rí- e-	tes,
7. *A fácie Dómini*	mo-	ta	est	ter-	ra,
8. *Qui convértit petram in*	sta-	gna	a-	quá-	rum,
10. *Super misericórdia tua et ve-*	ri-	tá-	te	tu-	a:
12. *Simulácra géntium ar-*	gén-	tum	et	au-	rum,
14. *Aures ha-*	bent	et	non	aú- di-	ent:
16. *Símiles illis fiant qui*	fá-	ci-	unt	e-	a:
18. *Domus Áaron spe-*	rá-	vit	in	Dó- mi-	no:
20. *Dóminus me-*	mor	fu-	it	no-	stri:
22. *Benedíxit ómnibus*	qui	ti-	ment	Dó- mi-	num,
24. *Benedí-*	cti	vos	a	Dó- mi-	no,
26. *Non mórtui lau-*	dá-	bunt	te	Dó- mi-	ne:
28. *Glória*	Pa-	tri	et	Fí- li-	o,

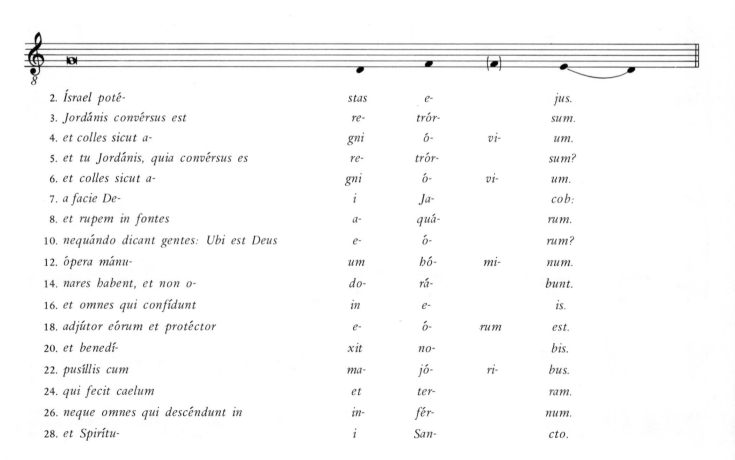

2. *Ísrael poté-*	stas	e-		jus.
3. *Jordánis convérsus est*	re-	trór-		sum.
4. *et colles sicut a-*	gni	ó-	vi-	um.
5. *et tu Jordánis, quia convérsus es*	re-	trór-		sum?
6. *et colles sicut a-*	gni	ó-	vi-	um.
7. *a facie De-*	i	Ja-		cob:
8. *et rupem in fontes*	a-	quá-		rum.
10. *nequándo dicant gentes: Ubi est Deus*	e-	ó-		rum?
12. *ópera mánu-*	um	hó-	mi-	num.
14. *nares habent, et non o-*	do-	rá-		bunt.
16. *et omnes qui confídunt*	in	e-		is.
18. *adjútor eórum et protéctor*	e-	ó-	rum	est.
20. *et benedí-*	xit	no-		bis.
22. *pusíllis cum*	ma-	jó-	ri-	bus.
24. *qui fecit caelum*	et	ter-		ram.
26. *neque omnes qui descéndunt in*	in-	fér-		num.
28. *et Spíritu-*	i	San-		cto.

[10] Miserere mei, Deus

ALCUNI VERSI DEL MISERERE sopra il falsobordone del DENTICE

Canto

Miserere   1. Miserére mei,   De-   us,   se-cún-dum ma-

-gnam mi- se- ri- cór- di-am tu-   -   am.

Basso
10

Quoniam   4. Quóniam iniquitátem meam   e-   -   go co-

-gnó-　　sco:　　et_____ pec- cá- tum me- um con- tra

me _____est ____ sem- - per.

Ecce　　7. Ecce enim veritátem di- le- xí-

-sti:　　incérta et occúlta sapiéntiae tuae manife- stá-

-sti___ mi- - hi.

Tenore

Averte　10. Avérte fáciem tuam a pec- cá- -

-tis me- is:　et o-

-mnes　i- ni- qui-tá- tes me- - as de-

le.

Canto
45

Redde   13. Redde mihi laetítiam   sa-   lu-   tá-

ris tu-   i:_____

50

et spíritu princi-   pá-   li

con- fír- ma me.

Domine 16. Dómine, lábia me- a a- pé-

-ri- es: et os me-

-um an-nun- ti- á- bit lau-

-dem _____ tu- _____ am.

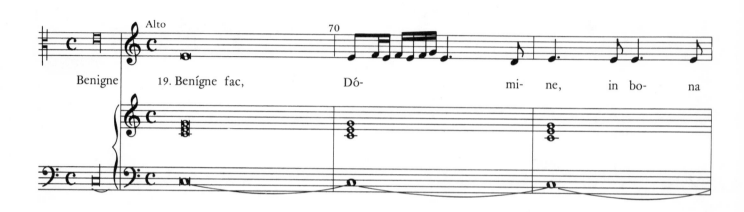

Benigne   19. Benígne fac,   Dó-   mi- ne, in bo-   na

vo- lun- tá- te tu-   - a _____ Si-   on:

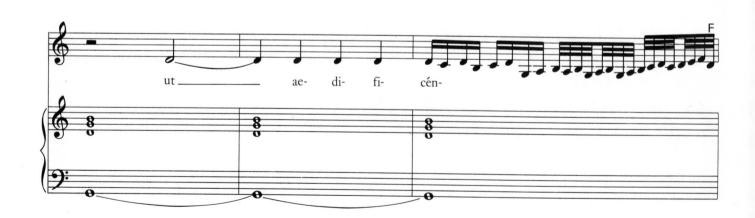

ut _____   ae- di- fi- cén-

-tur mu- ri Je- rú- - sa- lem.

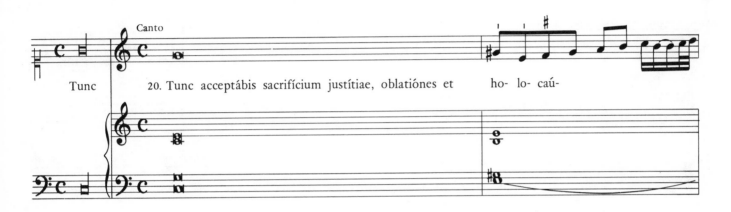

Tunc

20. Tunc acceptábis sacrifícium justítiae, oblatiónes et ho- lo- caú-

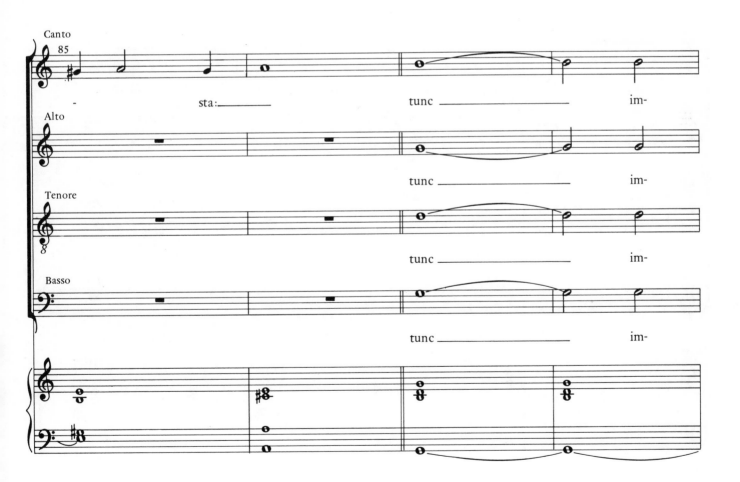

-sta: tunc im-

tunc im-

tunc im-

tunc im-

66

Chant verses for *alternatim* performance.

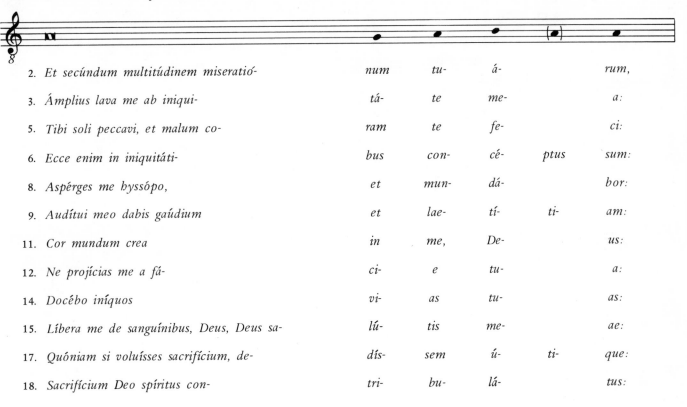

2. *Et secúndum multitúdinem miseratió-*	*num*	*tu-*	*á-*		*rum,*
3. *Ámplius lava me ab iniqui-*	*tá-*	*te*	*me-*		*a:*
5. *Tibi soli peccavi, et malum co-*	*ram*	*te*	*fe-*		*ci:*
6. *Ecce enim in iniquitáti-*	*bus*	*con-*	*cé-*	*ptus*	*sum:*
8. *Aspérges me hyssópo,*	*et*	*mun-*	*dá-*		*bor:*
9. *Audítui meo dabis gáudium*	*et*	*lae-*	*tí-*	*ti-*	*am:*
11. *Cor mundum crea*	*in*	*me,*	*De-*		*us:*
12. *Ne projícias me a fá-*	*ci-*	*e*	*tu-*		*a:*
14. *Docébo iníquos*	*vi-*	*as*	*tu-*		*as:*
15. *Líbera me de sanguínibus, Deus, Deus sa-*	*lú-*	*tis*	*me-*		*ae:*
17. *Quóniam si voluísses sacrifícium, de-*	*dís-*	*sem*	*ú-*	*ti-*	*que:*
18. *Sacrifícium Deo spíritus con-*	*tri-*	*bu-*	*lá-*		*tus:*

2. *dele ini-*	*qui-*	*tá-*	*tem*	*me-*	*am.*
3. *et a peccá-*	*to*	*me-*	*o*	*mún-*	*da me.*
5. *ut justificéris in sermónibus tuis, et vincas*	*cum*	*ju-*	*di-*	*cá-*	*ris.*
6. *et in peccátis concépit*	*me*	*ma-*	*ter*	*me-*	*a.*
8. *lavábis me, et super ni-*	*vem*	*de-*	*al-*	*bá-*	*bor.*
9. *et exsultábunt ossa*	*hu-*	*mi-*	*li-*	*á-*	*ta.*
11. *et spíritum rectum ínnova in vi-*	*scé-*	*ri-*	*bus*	*me-*	*is.*
12. *et spíritum sanctum tuum ne*	*aú-*	*fe-*	*ras*	*a*	*me.*
14. *et ímpii ad*	*te*	*con-*	*ver-*	*tén-*	*tur.*
15. *et exsultábit lingua mea ju-*	*stí-*	*ti-*	*am*	*tu-*	*am.*
17. *holocáustis*	*non*	*de-*	*le-*	*ctá-*	*be-ris.*
18. *cor contrítum, et humiliátum, De-*	*us,*	*non*	*de-*	*spí-*	*ci-es.*

APPENDICES

Appendix A: Miserere

Dentice
(*Lamentationi*, 1593)

[Miserére mei, De- us, se- cún- dum magnam misericórdiam tu- am.]

APPENDIX B: Miserere

Dentice
(Capp. Sist. Cod. 205, ca. 1630)

P.° C. [Primus Chorus] fer. 6. Denticis

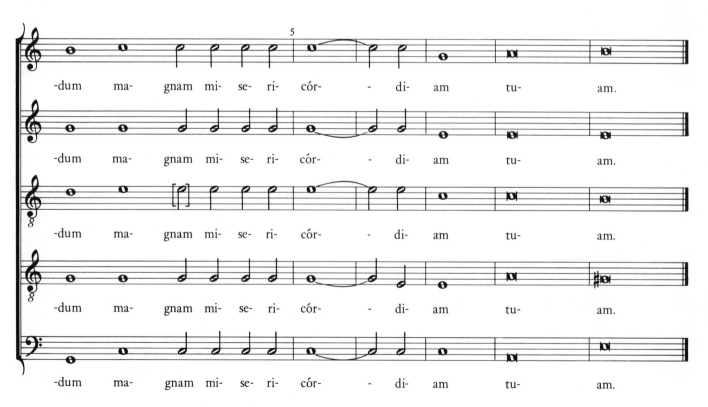

APPENDIX C: Miserere

Del Signor Fabritio Dentice

Donatiello Coya
(Responsorii, 1622)

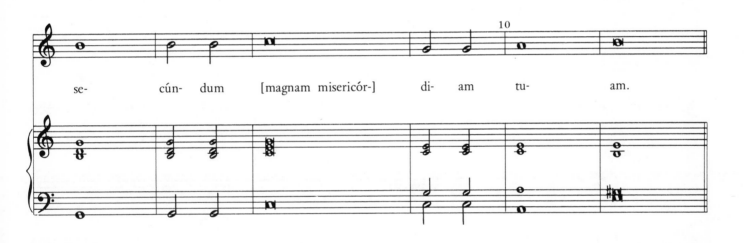

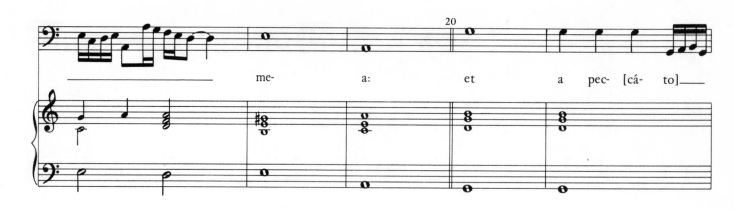

me- a: et a pec- [cá- to]

me- o mun- da me.

Di Donatiello Coya

Ecce   7. Ecce [enim veri-]   tá-   tem di- le-

- xí- sti: in- ceŕta [et occúlta sapiéntiae tu-]

in vi- scé- - ri- bus me- - - is.

[Tenor]

Quoniam 17. Quóniam [si voluísses sacrifícium, de-] dís- - sem

ú- ti- que: [ho- lo- caú- -

-stis non] de- le- ctá- - - be- ris.